THE DALA HORSE

Lissa Johnston

Lissa Johnston
721 Wildwood Rd.
Leesville, SC 29070

www.lissajohnston.com
lissajohnston@gmail.com
@lissa_johnston

Cover Design by www.ebooklaunch.com

ISBN: 0-9973068-2-3

ISBN-13: 978-0-9973068-2-8

For the intrepid Norwegian immigrants who chose Texas as their new home.

The Dala Horse

CHAPTER ONE

August 1867 Bosque County, Texas - The summer sun beat down on Kaya Olson's head as she dropped a handful of hard-baked earth onto the coffin six feet below. The rock-like clods shattered against the long wooden box, leaving a fine spray of gray dirt across its top. There were no coffins available when Sheriff Taylor brought word, none that met Papa's standards. The funeral was delayed until Papa could make one. And now, there it lay in a hole in the ground, with her mother inside. Friends and family passed by Kaya, depositing their own handfuls before they walked down the hill to the road back to Normandy. Finally, Kaya and her father were the only two left. "Time to go home, Kaya," Lars Olson said, turning away from the grave. Kaya only looked back once, struck by the different sound an entire shovelful of dirt made as it hit the pine.

1

As they approached their rented house on Church Street, mourners' wagons lined the road. Still-hitched horses stretched their necks to graze the neighbors' grass. Kaya's father expertly steered Old Ned between two of the wagons and into their side yard. "I'll move it when everyone goes home," he said, hopping down and starting around to her side of the wagon. She clambered down before he could help her. Warm breath and wet slobber grazed the back of her knees.

"Hello, Odin. Hey, boy, did you miss me?" Kaya knelt down and gave Odin a big hug. "I missed you, too." Odin's short tan fur was warm from the sun. Kaya inhaled his doggie aroma. The top of his head still smelled like a puppy – a 90-pound, 3-year-old mutt puppy. Kaya held him a little longer than usual. He wiggled out of her grasp and bounded ahead of her as she walked across the wilted grass toward the back door.

"Where are you going?" her father called as he unhitched Old Ned.

"In through the back, like always," she answered. "Only company comes in the front."

Kaya went to the cistern in the back yard and

dipped out some water. She ladled it into a pail sitting in the shade of the pecan tree so Odin could have a cold drink. Then she took a deep breath and stepped up onto the small back porch. Conversations mingled with the clink of dishware floated outside.

"Kaya, dear, don't just stand there! Come in out of the sun." *Onkel* Otto had a full plate in one hand and a glass of milk in the other. He elbowed open the screen door.

"*Takk, Onkel,*" she said as she squeezed by him.

"Kaya, Kaya, you poor thing," *Tante* Julia wailed as she crossed the small kitchen and wrapped Kaya in her arms. Kaya stood patiently and waited for the hug to end. Unlike other Norwegians she knew, *Tante* Julia insisted on a hug at every opportunity. "How are you holding up, dear? You're so pale. Are you feeling all right?"

"Of course she's not all right, Julia! She just buried her mother, for goodness sake."

"Oh hush, Otto, you know what I mean." *Tante* Julia released Kaya and stepped back. "Now you know if you ever need anything, just knock on our door. You can depend on me and your *Onkel* Otto. Anything at all, dear."

"*Takk,*" Kaya repeated, unable to think of anything

she would need, unless they could bring her mother back. Anxious to avoid more wailing and hugging, Kaya slipped through the kitchen, down the hall to her room, and shut the door.

Kaya's room was small but neat. The wallpaper was not Kaya's favorite, but she had grown accustomed to it. Huge blue hydrangeas sprawled across a background that might have been ivory once, but was now more like tan. The single bed's plain wood frame had been too tempting for her carpenter father. It was now ornately carved in a design traditional to his native Norway.

A sunbeam sliced across the quilt on her bed. Kaya was proud of that quilt. Different strips of light-colored fabric, about the length and width of her index finger, were sewn into a 'L' shape. Darker shades formed another, and together the pairs of 'L's formed a complex pattern of light and dark squares. Alma Olson had begun teaching her daughter how to sew when she was six. This was the first quilt she allowed Kaya to stitch on the quilting, not just the piecing. And that only came after hours of carding the cotton so it could be spun, then woven into fabric, then dyed. Kaya had spent even more time carding the seeds out of the cotton to be used as the batting. Her mother would not allow a single seed anywhere in her quilts.

Kaya ran a finger along her mother's stitches. They were skillfully made, tiny and uniform, at least ten to the inch without fail. Quilting was the only social activity Kaya's mother had enjoyed. She usually found ways to avoid the Norwegian community in Normandy. This was impressive considering five out of the six houses on their street were occupied by Norwegians. "Meddlers," she would say. "Kaya, when you are grown, be sure to keep your nose out of other people's business."

Kaya lay down and stared at the ceiling, still dry-eyed. She wasn't sure why, but she hadn't been able to cry. *I'm sorry, Mama.*

Kaya is at home in the back yard, throwing a stick to Odin. He is tired of playing fetch and wants her to chase him instead. He stops in front of her, just out of reach, and extends his front paws forward, rump in the air, chest almost touching the ground. He shakes the stick side to side and growls his playful growl. She plays along, grabbing for the stick. This goes on for a few minutes until

Odin springs up and dashes away. He stops and turns, waiting for her to follow. They play a wild game of chase. Kaya stops beneath the kitchen window to catch her breath, her hands on her knees. As she stoops over, panting, she hears voices from inside her house - her mother and Tante Julia. They sound angry.

"Will you look after her or not, Julia?"

*"You know I will. But **you** are her mother. Your place is here with her, not running all over the countryside by yourself. No respectable woman travels alone."*

"What would you have me do? Olena is ill and Lars is away."

"Olena Olson ill? What nonsense. Alma, you are playing a dangerous game."

"Talk about nonsense – just listen to yourself. Your boring life in this boring town makes your imagination run wild. It's a simple visit to my mother-in-law. Lars will be back soon, Julia. Kaya won't be a burden to you for long."

"How can such a pretty face say such ugly things, Alma? You know we love Kaya like she was our own."

Odin is tired of waiting for her to return to their game. He starts barking. Kaya whispers as loud as she dares for him to be quiet, but it is too late. She jumps at her mother's voice.

> *"Kaya! Is that you out there?*
>
> *"Yes, Mama."*
>
> *"Come inside this minute."*

Kaya awoke, her heart pounding from the dream. Only it wasn't a dream. It happened a few days before her mother died. She was glad she woke up before the rest of the scene played itself out. Her mother had been angry and irritable before she left. Kaya assumed it was because she thought Kaya was eavesdropping that day. A cold tangle of regret returned to its hiding place in her stomach.

She lay quietly, blinking away the sleep. It took a moment for her to remember why she was still fully dressed in her good navy blue church dress. Then despair settled over her like the light sheet someone had covered her with during her nap. Kaya sat up, swinging her legs over the edge of the bed, and listened. The house was much quieter now. The scent of fresh-baked yeast rolls and something else – *kjøtboller* ? – set her stomach growling. *Maybe they've all gone.* Then, voices drifted down the hallway. Her father was talking with someone in the front room.

"It's so soon, Lars!" a man's voice said.

"It's the perfect time," rumbled her father.

"What about Kaya?"

Kaya opened her door just enough to hear the rest of the conversation. Her conscience told her it was wrong to eavesdrop, but she ignored it when she heard her name. She tiptoed down the hall to the front of the house. *Who was Papa talking to?*

"What about her?"

"This is her home. Her school, her friends-"

"She will make new friends," her father answered curtly.

Silence. Then the other person continued, "Well, I suppose there is nothing to keep you here, now that Alma-"

"Yes," her father interrupted.

"I'm sorry, Lars. It's just that it all seems so sudden."

Kaya recognized the other voice. It was Pastor Swenson. Before she could change her mind, she stepped into the parlor. "Hello, Pastor."

Pastor Swenson sloshed his coffee onto the table. He pulled his handkerchief from his pocket and began swiping at it before it could drip onto the floor. "Well, ahem, um, hello there, Kaya." He continued mopping up and gave her father a knowing look.

"How long have you been standing there, Kaya? You know it's not polite to eavesdrop."

"I wasn't, Papa. I woke up and heard voices. I just wanted to see who was still here."

Lars Olson frowned. Pastor Swenson rose to break the uncomfortable silence. "I was just leaving. I know it has been a long day for both of you."

"That was a fine service, Pastor," Lars said. "I am thankful you happened to be here this week."

"I will be here another week before I head to Brownsboro" the minister said. "Please let me know if there is anything I can do. I will remember you in my prayers."

"Thank you, Pastor." Lars Olson rose and the men shook hands. Pastor Swenson collected his bible and his hat and made his exit.

Before her mother died, Kaya could not remember the last time she had been alone with her father. He was away fighting in the war for nearly two years. When he returned, his carpentry jobs kept him away for days at a time. Even when he had jobs in Normandy, often he was gone by the time she woke up and did not return until supper. The three of them attended church together, took meals together, but rarely was her father around when her mother wasn't.

Kaya drifted to the room's window. Out in the front yard, Odin rose from the shade of the front porch and watched Pastor Swenson walk away. Still looking out the front window, she said, "What seems so sudden, Papa?"

"What?"

"Pastor Swenson said, 'it all seems so sudden'."

"So you were listening, after all."

Kaya turned to face him. "I'm sorry. I could hear you all the way down the hall."

He gestured to one of the chairs. "Come sit, Kaya. We need to talk." Kaya chose the chair directly across from her father's place on the sofa.

Grandpa Olson's clock ticked loudly on the table behind Kaya. Lars rested his forearms on his knees and looked at the floor with a great sigh. At last he raised his head and said, "How are you holding up, Kaya?"

"Fine, Papa."

"Now that your mother is gone, we will have to be strong together."

"I know, Papa."

He looked away from her. "Things will be different now."

"Yes, Papa."

Kaya's empty stomach gurgled.

"Have you eaten anything today?"

"Sir?"

"Have you eaten?"

"No, Papa."

"You need to eat something." He got up and headed back to the kitchen. "Come on. We can finish our talk in the kitchen."

The kitchen table groaned with the bounty of generous friends and relatives. Lars pulled away the cotton sheet protecting the mountain of food from any flies that may have found their way inside the house. All manner of crockery held pies, *lefse*, vegetables, and meats. Sure enough, there were the meatballs she had smelled earlier. Kaya's father retrieved a clean plate from the cupboard and started serving her. He noticed her stare. "Kaya, just because the only thing you have ever seen me do in this room is eat, doesn't mean I don't know my way around the kitchen." He paused with a plate in one hand, serving spoon in the other. "Potatoes? Green beans? How about a drumstick?"

"Yes, that's fine, Papa. That's plenty."

He pushed aside a deep dish apple pie and held a chair until she sat, then took a seat opposite her and waited until she ate a few bites. "Kaya, I have made plans for us."

Kaya swallowed a mouthful of mashed potatoes. "Plans?"

"Now that your mother is gone, I will need someone to help me look after you."

"What about *Tante* Julia and *Onkel* Otto?"

"We are not talking about helping out a little here and there, Kaya. We'll need help with everything, every day. Especially when my work takes me away from home."

"Yes, like when Mama died."

Lars frowned. Then he continued, "When your *Bestefar* Olson died last year, that left your *Bestemor* Olson alone to work their ranch. She has a sharecropper, but it's still too much for her to manage. She is much too old to have to worry about such a large job. Now that your mother – now that things are different for us, I think it would be best for us to go live with *Bestemor* Olson. You see? We can help each other."

Kaya stared at her father. "Live with her? Doesn't she live in Preston? That's miles and miles from here."

"Yes, that's true. It is three days' journey by wagon."

"But what about school? My friends? What about *Tante* Julia and *Onkel* Otto?"

"There are plenty of children in Preston. You will meet them when school starts up again after the harvest. They have a fine teacher there. . .", he said, his voice drifting off with his gaze. He blinked, then continued. "*Tante* Julia and *Onkel* Otto can come visit whenever they like. I know it has been a long time since you saw your *Bestemor*. She didn't want to travel during the war, and then when *Bestefar* Olson . . . when he died, well, she didn't feel it was safe for a woman her age to travel alone."

"Because of the Americans?"

"Americans?"

"After *Bestefar* Olson died, you told me to be careful around town. You said to stay away from the Americans, because the war turned some of them into bandits."

"Kaya, that was years ago."

"But you were right. You and *Bestemor* were both

right."

"Right? About what?"

"Didn't bandits kill Mama?"

"It looks like it, yes."

"Wasn't she traveling alone?"

Lars sighed but said nothing. When her father didn't answer, Kaya continued. "Are there many Americans in Preston?"

"I suppose so."

"More than here?"

"Yes."

"Are there any other Norwegians besides *Bestemor*?"

"A few. Not as many as here."

"What-"

Her father cut her off. "That's enough questions, Kaya."

"I won't know anyone. The Americans will make fun of me, and call me 'Norskie'. I won't go!"

"Kaya!" Lars said sharply, smacking his hand on the table. Kaya jumped. As the sound faded, her father got control of himself before he continued. Speaking more softly, he said, "I'm sorry. I know all of this is hard for you. This is difficult for all of us. But I must do this if we are to survive. So many people have come to Texas since the war ended. It is harder to find work. But there is work in Preston. They are building a new school. I know the man in charge. He is Norwegian, like us. I had already made arrangements to work on this job before your mother died, and he is expecting me. Leaving you here with *Tante* Julia and *Onkel* Otto is out of the question. You'll come to Preston with me and stay with *Bestemor*. And I can help *Bestemor* with her ranch. It is high time I took responsibility and helped her, now that your mother . . . now that *Bestefar* is gone."

Kaya took a deep breath. "This is all my fault."

"What is your fault?"

"Having to move away from Normandy. If Mama hadn't gotten on that stage coach that got robbed, she wouldn't have gotten shot." She hadn't meant to confess any of this to anyone, least of all her father. But once she started, the words tumbled out of her. "And if Mama hadn't gotten mad at me the day before she left, maybe she wouldn't have gone," she continued, her voice quavering. "We wouldn't be moving. And Mama would still be alive." Giving voice to what had been eating away at her, saying it out loud, had a curious effect. A flood of pent-up tears began to flow. She crossed her arms on the table in front of her, shoving her plate willy-nilly, and lay her head down and cried.

"Oh, Kaya." Lars walked around the table. At first he stood awkwardly. As Kaya's tears lessened, he knelt so that he was at her level. "Listen to me. This is not your fault. Your mama didn't leave because she was mad at you. Where did you get such an idea?"

"Yes, she did," Kaya's response was muffled by her arms. She sniffed and sat up. "The day before she left, I was playing outside with Odin, and the windows were open. Mama saw me, and she got angry because she thought I heard her and *Tante* Julia talking. I did hear, sort of, but it was an accident. Mama told *Tante* Julia she would be glad to get away from Normandy for a while." Kaya sniffed again. Lars handed her a napkin and she wiped her nose.

"Kaya, I think you must have mis-heard her. Your mama told *Tante* Julia she was going to visit *Bestemor* Olson because she got word *Bestemor* has been ill. Her leaving had nothing to do with you. And if *Bestemor* is sick, that's another reason we need to go to Preston."

Kaya shook her head. "No, Papa. That's what I heard Mama and *Tante* Julia arguing about. *Tante* Julia said *Bestemor* is never sick. If she's never sick, then Mama must have left because of me." Tears threatened again, but Kaya bit the inside of her cheek to hold them in check.

Lars Olson frowned. "It is true your *Bestemor* is a very healthy woman. She has survived two fever epidemics since coming to America. But everyone gets sick now and then. We will find out when we see her. I don't know about this business with *Bestemor*, but one thing I do know for sure: your mama's death is *not your fault*." Lars tilted Kaya's chin up until she met his eyes. "Understand?"

"Yes, sir." Kaya answered automatically. She looked down again when Lars stood back up. "May I be excused?"

He took in her plate, her tear-stained face. "You didn't eat much."

"I'm not hungry, Papa."

Closing the door behind her, Kaya headed into the back yard. Her head was spinning. She was desperate to get outside, to think. Locusts burred in the sultry evening air. Their familiar rhythm calmed her as she slipped away from the back porch and over to the pecan tree. It was her thinking spot. Her father had built a simple bench, long enough for two or three of someone her size to sit and enjoy the shade. With his help, she had painted it white, and it glowed in the early dusk. Leaning against the ancient tree, she pulled her knees up to her chest and closed her eyes.

Odin's wet tongue swiped across the back of her hand. She patted the bench beside her and he leaped up gracefully to join her. Then he plopped down on his side with his head in her lap. She stroked his fur and watched the stars come out as they always had, as if nothing had changed.

But things *were* changing, much too fast. She remembered happier times, before Sheriff Taylor had brought his grim news. Papa said it wasn't her fault, but of course he would say that. She wanted to believe him. But she needed more than her Papa's reassurances. She needed answers. And if Papa was right, and her mother's death wasn't her fault, whose fault was it?

CHAPTER TWO

One week after the funeral, Kaya sat on the front porch and watched her father, *Onkel* Otto, and Pastor Swenson finish loading their wagon. She felt as empty as their house. Her father had let the other Norwegians in town know they were leaving. All of their belongings were packed. Now all that was left to do was go.

The posts of her parents' (*father's*, now) headboard protruded from the loaded wagon like the horns on Mr. Anderson's prize bull. Her own smaller bed and trunk were in there somewhere, along with the down bedding. *Tante* Julia had helped her pack their few dishes, pans and kitchen utensils into a straw-filled crate. Her father's trunk sat at the back of the wagon. Its leather straps were belted tightly as if to say, 'Nothing else is going into or coming out of here'.

Lars Olson shoved one last crate in to the back of the wagon. He spotted one of his saws sticking out of his

19

work satchel and took a moment to secure it. *Onkel* Otto leaned against the wagon, sweating heavily in the afternoon heat.

"Is that everything, Lars?" Pastor Swenson asked, mopping his brow with a faded blue handkerchief. He was going part of the way to Preston with them since he was due back in Brownsboro soon.

Saw, satchel, and wagon now packed to his liking, Lars nodded once decisively. He noticed Kaya on the porch. "Kaya, go through the house and see if there is anything we have forgotten. Take your time. If we leave anything behind, it may be a long time before we can come back and get it."

"Yes, Papa." Kaya walked back inside. To her left, the sitting room looked much as it always had. It still contained a sofa, two chairs, a table and some lamps. When they rented this house across the street from *Onkel* Otto and *Tante* Julia, it was partially furnished. A few telltale dusty outlines told her *Bestefar* Olson's clock, a chair her father had made, and a woven rug were already packed on the wagon. As she glanced into her parents' (*father's, now*) bedroom to her right, the large trunk sitting there in the middle of the floor was hard to miss. Her mother's trunk! It was unlatched, its leather straps dangling down the front. How could her father have overlooked it?

Kaya's mother was a young girl when her family, the Piersons, immigrated from Norway to Texas. The trunk had made the long, dangerous trip across the ocean and overland with her. Dark with aged varnish, it bore many miles of wear, many years of service to her family. A large bouquet of plump painted flowers spread across the top. Leaves and vines curled outward. Once brightly colored, the flowers now faded softly into the wood. Kaya rubbed a finger along its edge. She unbuckled its straps and lifted the lid back gently so that it would not suddenly flop back down on her fingers.

Her mother's clothing lay inside, neatly folded, smelling faintly of violets (*Mama!*). The inside of the trunk was lined with faded beige paper decorated with tiny pale pink rosebuds. It bore some water stains and was peeling off in a few places. Sheriff Taylor had returned the trunk when he brought her mother's body back to Normandy. Its contents were perfectly organized, nothing like her mother's slap-dash style. Kaya wondered if *Tante* Julia re-packed it. She couldn't imagine her father being so particular about handling women's things. Tools, yes.

Dresses, no.

"Kaya?" *Tante* Julia said from the doorway. She came in and stood beside Kaya, looking into the trunk. "Your mama had so many lovely things. Now they are yours. Take good care of them, Kaya. Some, like her *bunad*, might be hard to replace here in America. You don't want to lose it. Maybe you will wear it on your wedding day." *Tante* Julia winked.

Kaya couldn't imagine meeting anyone in Preston that she would like, much less marry. But she kept that thought to herself. "I will. *Tante* Julia, is this everything of Mama's?"

"Why, yes, I suppose it is."

"If Mama was just going to visit *Bestemor* Olson, why did she take this big trunk? She had a travel satchel her parents gave her when she married Papa."

Tante Julia's eyebrows knit together. Before she could answer, Lars strode into the room.

"What are you two doing?" He frowned at the opened trunk.

"Just looking at Mama's trunk, Papa.." Kaya lifted the lid and began to latch it closed.

"Good. We're all finished packing the wagon. We

need to be going." He turned to leave.

"Papa?" Kaya said. "Aren't you forgetting something?" She fed the last leather strap through its buckle and stood.

Lars cocked an eyebrow.

Kaya patted the trunk to give him a hint. When he didn't respond, she said, "Mama's trunk. You need to put it on the wagon."

"On the wagon?" he replied. "We're not taking it. We don't have room."

"Papa!" Kaya cried. "Mama's good green dress, her *bunad*, her quilts -" Kaya turned to her aunt, then back to her father. "We can't leave Mama's trunk!"

"There, there." *Tante* Julia patted Kaya's back. In the same comforting tone, she said, "Lars, really – a few items of Alma's, to make it easier for her. If you can make room in the wagon, what's the harm?"

Lars shoved his hands in his pockets and looked at his feet. Kaya held her breath. Finally, he gave in. "All right. I will go make more room." In one fluid movement he knelt, grabbed the leather handle at one end and hoisted the trunk onto his broad back. Just like that, it was gone, and the room was empty save for *Tante* Julia and Kaya.

"Thank you," Kaya said softly.

Tante Julia took Kaya's hand and gave it a gentle squeeze. "You're welcome, child. Now let's finish cleaning, and we can go to my house for a nice supper."

A large calloused hand gently shook Kaya's shoulder. "Time to get up, Kaya," her father said. "Time for some breakfast before we get on the road."

Kaya blinked. Her father's boots filled her vision for a moment, then were replaced by the whitewashed boards of Otto and Julia's back porch rail. *Tante* Julia had spread a pallet on their back porch for her to sleep on. A quilt was tangled around her feet. She sat up and rubbed her eyes. Odin barked at her from the pre-dawn gloom in the back yard. He was eating something *Tante* Julia tossed out to him for his breakfast. From the delicious smells coming from the kitchen, it was some sort of pork.

"Good morning, Kaya!" greeted *Tante* Julia as Kaya came through the back door. "Just in time before these two gobble up everything!"

Kaya's father and Onkel Otto sat at the kitchen table, which was barely visible under all the food set out.

One large tray held more scrambled eggs than Kaya had ever seen. Another was filled with fresh biscuits packed tightly together and glistening with butter. *Onkel* Otto was busy applying honey to his biscuits – his second helping by the look of his plate. Her father sipped some of *Tante* Julia's coffee and leaned back in his chair, his plate empty but for a few crumbs.

"Who else is coming to breakfast?" Kaya asked.

"Just Pastor Swenson," her father said.

"What's your pleasure, Miss Olson?" At the stove *Tante* Julia held a utensil in each hand. The left hand turned the bacon, while the right hand whisked the porridge.

Kaya's appetite had returned after several days of not having one. "Porridge, please," Kaya answered as she pulled up a chair.

"Porridge it is," answered *Tante* Julia. "I think I will join you. When I was a girl like you, before we came to America, I thought if I never ate another bowl of porridge in my whole life it would be too soon. But now that I am old –"

"You're not old, *Tante* Julia!" Kaya protested.

"Forty next spring," *Tante* Julia replied. "And now

I find that I sometimes miss my Norwegian porridge after all." She passed a plate of bacon to the table, then brought the two bowls and sat. As Kaya reached for her spoon, *Tante* Julia said, "Wait!" and daubed a generous helping of butter on top. "Now it's ready! Oh, and Lars, that basket over there is full of food to eat on your trip. Don't forget it, or you will be hunting squirrels for your dinner."

Kaya's eyes grew wide. "Mama says squirrels are troll food," she said, before she remembered her mama would not be saying that any more. She got a lump in her throat.

Tante Julia squeezed Kaya's shoulder. "Yes, your mama, bless her, did not care for squirrel, that is true."

"Squirrel isn't bad," *Onkel* Otto said after a moment. "A little potato, some carrots, and you have yourself a nice stew." He helped himself to more bacon. "Does Olena still keep her big garden, with all of those fresh melons and pumpkins?"

"I suppose she does," said Lars, resuming his meal. "Beans, carrots, turnips – *Mor* loves her garden."

Onkel Otto said, "Don't forget her plums. Kaya, your grandmother grows some of the best plums in Van Zandt county." He reached for another biscuit. "Pass the butter, please."

"Come in, Johan," *Tante* Julia called after a knock sounded on the front door. Pastor Swenson entered. He greeted everyone and took the empty chair next to Kaya's father. *Tante* Julia slid a heaping plate of eggs, bacon and biscuits in front of him before he had a chance to say anything but, "*Mange takk!*"

"*Vær så god!*" *Tante* Julia answered, and joined the group at the table. The adults chatted companionably as they enjoyed their hearty meal.

After Lars mopped the last of the cream gravy from his plate with a bite of biscuit, he pushed back from the table. "This was a wonderful meal, but we must be going, Julia," he said. "I would like to get to our first stop before dark."

Suddenly everyone was up bustling about. *Tante* Julia retrieved the basket of food for their trip. Kaya moved to help her do the dishes, but her aunt shooed her out the front door behind the men. Outside, Old Ned was already hitched up and ready to go.

Kaya stopped. A second horse stood patiently in the morning gloom, its reins attached to the back of the wagon.

"What's wrong?"

"Nothing, Papa. I just forgot we were taking Dala."

"Of course we are taking Dala. She's a fine animal. She'll manage this trip better than all of us."

Dala was Kaya's mother's horse. Alma Olson loved riding. She had begun teaching Kaya to ride. It was Kaya's favorite time with her mother. When Alma was around horses, her love for them overflowed to everything around her, including Kaya. Kaya was a little frightened of horses. They were so big, and she was so far off the ground sitting in that saddle. To Kaya's surprise, despite her fears, she was getting the hang of riding. She worked hard to conceal her trepidation. A part of her knew Alma wouldn't understand. Spending such pleasant times with her mother had been worth a few butterflies in her stomach.

Lars had purchased the pony two years ago from the local blacksmith. He claimed he needed an extra work horse, but Dala was too small for much work. Kaya knew he really bought Dala just to please her mother. And Alma was definitely pleased with the little sorrel. She rode Dala nearly every day. "It's not proper, riding around by herself like that," Kaya heard Mrs. Clausen say in the pew behind her at church one Sunday. Mrs. Clausen was hard of hearing. She talked louder than she realized. But Alma

Olson didn't much care what others thought of her.

While Lars gave Old Ned's harness one final check, *Tante* Julia hugged Kaya tightly. Kaya's eyes grew watery at the thought of leaving her and *Onkel* Otto. When *Tante* Julia saw this, her own flood gates opened and she wept unashamedly, shoulders heaving, for a good minute. *Onkel* Otto patted his wife's back and sniffed into an enormous red handkerchief. At last, *Tante* Julia wiped her eyes with her damp apron. With a final hug, she reminded Kaya to be sure and write. *Onkel* Otto then helped Kaya into the wagon.

Kaya scooted over and patted the seat beside her. "Come on, boy." Odin made an impressive leap up to the seat. He took a quick look around and settled himself on top of the crates behind Kaya. Finally, her father climbed up and took the reins.

"*Adjø,* Otto," he said as he reached down to shake hands.

"*Adjø,* Lars." *Onkel* Otto grasped Lars' outstretched hand with both of his. "Safe journey to both of you. We hope to see you again soon."

"Yes, of course," said Lars. "I don't know how to thank you."

"Never mind," said Otto. "Happy to do it. You three better get going."

Lars nodded and touched his broad-brimmed hat in salute. He flicked the reins and clicked twice to Old Ned. The wagon lurched gently forward.

"*Adjø!*" Kaya called out. She waved madly until the road curved out of sight of the two figures waving back. Odin even barked a few times.

Their wagon creaked through the quiet of Normandy's early hours. They passed the post office and the general store, both still shuttered closed. On Kaya's right, a lone wagon wheel leaned against the hitching post in front of the blacksmith's shop. The smith waved to them as he prepared his fire for the day's hot work. Kaya wondered if he also waved to her mother's stage on the day she died. As they left town, Kaya feared they were leaving behind any chance for her to find answers to the questions that nagged her about her mother's death. She turned around and searched for the little hilltop cemetery where her mother remained behind. She could barely see it, but she knew in her heart where it was.

CHAPTER THREE

The first day on the road was uneventful, other than the excitement of the wagon and horses splashing through the shallow Brazos River crossing at Fort Graham. Kaya wasn't sure if she was more relieved or disappointed that she did not see any Indians there. Few other travelers passed them before they stopped for the night in Hillsboro. Day two at least brought some brief excitement with the appearance of a stage coach barreling toward them, trailed by a billowing cloud of dust. Lars guided their wagon well clear off to the side of the road into the prairie to let them pass. He and Pastor Swenson dug for their handkerchiefs and secured them over their noses and mouths. Lars handed one to Kaya and motioned for her to protect herself also.

Four sweating horses harnessed two-by-two hauled the stage along at a fair clip. It clattered noisily, bouncing and squeaking with a full load. One passenger hung his elbow out one of the open windows. Silhouettes of several other passengers swayed inside. Boxes, trunks and other luggage lay strapped to the top and rear of the coach. The driver and his seat mate glared in their direction. At the last moment, the second man begrudged them a tipped hat as they rolled by. But one hand remained on the long gun sitting across his lap. Kaya wondered why they were so wary, until she remembered the three of them wore bandanas over their faces.

Kaya's thoughts swirled like the dust in the stage's wake. Until now, her only image of her mother's death was that of her lifeless body contained within the pine coffin her father had made. But the sight of the coach fired her imagination about her mother's final moments. Those passengers were no different than her mother – unsuspecting travelers on their way to visit relatives, not realizing how quickly their lives could change forever. Questions bubbled over in her mind and began spilling out.

"Papa, why were there so many people on that stage? Don't they know how dangerous it is?" Kaya turned and watched the stage as it disappeared into the distance.

"It's not dangerous, Kaya," Lars said, reading her thoughts. "Your mama was just unlucky."

"But what about bandits? And Indians?"

"Bandits and Indians!" Pastor Swenson said. "Where on earth did you hear such talk?"

"Isn't that why Mama died, Papa? Because of American bandits?"

"Kaya, there are good and bad people everywhere," Lars said. "Good Americans, bad Americans, good Norwegians, bad Norwegians. What happened to your mama was a terrible thing. But people travel all over this state safely every day."

Pastor Swenson agreed. "I travel this route often, Kaya. What happened to your mother was the first time a stage coach has been robbed in these parts in many years. And as for Indians, I've made this trip twice a year the past two years and have never seen one."

"But – what about Ole Foss?"

"Ole Foss, well, that was unfortunate," Lars said. "We don't have to worry about Indians this far east."

"That man on the stage coach had his gun out," Kaya persisted. "Why would he have his gun out unless he thought something bad might happen?"

Lars and Pastor Swenson exchanged a look. "Sharp eyes, Kaya," Lars said. "He's riding shotgun. It's his job to protect the stage coach. Coaches don't always have someone riding shotgun unless they are expecting trouble. He might have been there to help guard something they were carrying."

"Carrying? Like what?"

"Stage coaches carry more than passengers. They also transport mail, and sometimes gold or cash from one bank to another. They have a special box called a 'strong box' under the driver's seat for valuables."

"Did Mama's coach have someone riding shotgun?"

Lars paused before answering, "Yes."

"Then why didn't he protect her? Isn't that his job?"

"He did. That is, he tried. Sheriff Taylor said the stage was robbed somewhere east of Hillsboro. There was a shootout. The guard hit one of the bandits and they scattered. So he did his job. They didn't succeed in robbing the stage. But your mother got caught in the crossfire. Do you understand? It was an accident."

"Will bandits rob us, too?"

"I don't know why they would. I don't think we have anything they want."

"What do they want?"

"Money, usually. Sometimes other things, if it's

something that's easy to transport and can be used as money or sold to get more money."

By lunchtime on their third day of travel they had splashed across another river, the Trinity. When they came to the small town of Goshen soon afterward, Pastor Swenson took his leave. "Head north here and you'll be at Preston by suppertime," he said, indicating the left fork in the road. "I'm headed straight on to Brownsboro. Give your mother my regards. Tell her I'll give them to her in person on my way back to Normandy in a few weeks."

As they watched him depart, Lars said, "Since we're stopped, would you like to ride Dala for a while? I'll saddle her for you."

Kaya eyed the sorrel. "I don't think so, Papa."

"Why not? I thought you would enjoy a little exercise after sitting in this wagon for two days."

"Kaya, what's the matter?"

"Nothing, Papa. I was just thinking about Mama. She sure loved her horse, didn't she?"

"Yes, I suppose she did." Lars flicked the reins. "How is your riding coming along?"

"I can ride. I can put Mama's little saddle on Dala

all by myself, if there's a stool for me to stand on. But Dala knows I'm not Mama. I'm not sure she'd let me ride her now that . . . now that Mama's gone."

"'Let' you ride her?" Lars looked sharply at Dala, then back at Kaya. "Has she tried to buck you off?"

"No, but . . . "

"But what?"

Kaya lifted one shoulder in half a shrug.

"Dala's a smart horse, Kaya," her father said. "She knows something's not right. But she'll get used to things eventually. And you'll feel like riding her again soon."

Soon the road turned and the Goshen crossing behind them was out of sight. Endless prairie spread in every direction. She didn't realize how much she had been counting on Pastor Swenson's navigational skills. "Papa, how will we know where to go, now that Pastor Swenson is gone?"

"Don't worry, Kaya. We're close enough now that we could find our way there in the dark if we had to." Noting her look of alarm, he added, "But we won't. It's simple. Preston is north of here, as Pastor Swenson said. We just head north until we run into it." When she didn't laugh, he continued, "We can't get lost as long as we know two things: what direction the place is that we want to find, and what direction we are heading. Put those two things together, and we will get there. Preston is north of us. We are heading north right now."

Kaya glanced around them. Nothing but rolling Texas prairie and summer sunshine. "How do you know?"

"Simple. The sun comes up in the east," Lars pointed to his right, "every day. Sets in the west," and he pointed to his left, "every day. That's one thing in this life you can count on for sure. And while we're at it, you might as well learn the other two directions. North is to your left if you are facing the rising sun. South is to your right. Just the opposite if you are facing a setting sun which would be facing . . . " He waited for her to answer.

"West?"

"Correct."

Kaya looked up. "What if the sun is in the middle, not rising and not setting? How do you know which way you are going?"

"If it's right above, you best be headed home for lunch." When Kaya didn't respond to his joke, he said, "You just have to wait and see which direction it moves."

"What if it's cloudy and you can't see the sun?

What if it's nighttime?"

"Well, if it's night, you can tell if you know your stars. Depends on what time of year. The stars move through the sky, just like the sun. If it's cloudy, that's a tough one. Just try not to get caught in unfamiliar territory on a cloudy night."

CHAPTER FOUR

As long as Pastor Swenson had been with them, he and Kaya's father talked of many adult topics, leaving Kaya free to read or nap or daydream or play with Odin. Now that it was just Kaya and her father, attempts at casual conversation dried up as quickly as the occasional creek beds they passed. Her father had nothing further to add about her mother's death, other than assuring Kaya she was not to blame. He dismissed her concerns about who they might run into on their journey and refused to discuss the topic of bandits any further. After fielding many of her questions about Ole Foss's kidnapping by Indians, that subject was also banned. But the carpenter in him was eager to point out the various types of trees they passed – the bois d'arc with its inedible fruit resembling oversized green apples; the pecan with its delicious nuts; the thorny mesquite. Despite Kaya's fears about bandits and Indians, by the end of the day the thing she was most afraid of was being bored to death. Their journey jolting over the rolling prairies of eastern Texas was long, hot and dry. The only things that crossed their path were a few rabbits by ground and hawks and vultures by air.

Following Odin's example, Kaya found napping was the best way to pass the time. Just when she thought they would never arrive, they did.

"I see it!" Kaya said.

"Your eyes are sharp," said her father. The two of them swayed and bounced along on the wagon seat as Old Ned plodded down the dirt road. "What do you think?"

What first appeared as a gray blur on the darkening horizon was now a rectangular building complete with chimney. It sat alone on the vast prairie. Kaya remembered their cozy home near the center of Normandy. Dozens of neighbors, the school, the town square – all were within easy walking distance. Kaya's stomach churned as a wave of homesickness struck. "It's bigger than I thought," she managed.

"I think there will be enough room for all of us," said her father. "Come on, old boy," he said to Ned. "A little further and you can have a nice cold drink of water and some oats for your hard work today." The sun had set, and they were arriving barely in time to be able to unhitch Old Ned without needing a lantern.

As they approached the cabin, a figure emerged. "Lars, is that you?" a woman's voice called.

"Yes, *Mor*, it's me. Don't shoot!" Lars replied. Kaya thought he was joking until she saw the unmistakable outline of a long-barreled gun dangling from the crook in the woman's elbow.

Lars pulled on the reins, much to Old Ned's relief. The resulting sway forward, then back, awoke Odin from his nap. He glanced around and sniffed the air before getting up to stretch. Then he jumped down and trotted off on some unknown bit of dog business.

"I see you got my letter," Lars said as he hopped down.

"Yes, Knud Jensen brought it by on his way to Tyler," she said, leaning her shotgun against the porch. She approached the wagon and peered up at Kaya. "This is little Kaya? *Velkommen, velkommen!*"

Kaya hesitated, then climbed down.

"My, how you've grown. You're almost up to my shoulder!" Olena Olson said, taking Kaya's hands in hers. "Do you remember me, child?"

Kaya glanced at her father before saying, "Yes, of course, *Bestemor*." But she didn't, not really. Olena and her husband had visited them in Normandy when Kaya was small, but Kaya hadn't seen them since before the war.

"Hmm. I wonder." Olena's mouth twitched as she tried to conceal a smile. Continuing her warm grasp of Kaya's hands, she leaned a little closer and said, "I was so sorry to hear about your mother. You are most welcome in my home." Kaya nodded her thanks as she had so many times those first few days after her mother's death. Olena nodded back and released her hands. "Come inside before the mosquitoes carry us away. I have made a stew, hoping you would be here some time in the next day or two."

"You two go ahead, *Mor*. I want to see to the horses."

Olena smiled and draped an arm across Kaya's shoulders as the two of them approached the Olson home.

Because Olena lived in the country, Kaya expected her to live in one of the crude log cabins she had read about. But this house was similar to her own home in Normandy. It was made of horizontal wood planks and had glass windows, a shingled roof, and a second chimney she hadn't noticed earlier. The home was simple in design. It appeared to be two identical houses a few feet apart, mirror images of each other. A single large roof covered both as if they were one big house. Kaya and Olena entered the long narrow space running between the two structures.

"You and your father will be living here," Olena said, pointing to the right half of the house. "It has been vacant ever since my hired girl left me and went back home to Louisiana. We will get you both settled in after dinner."

They entered a large, comfortable room through a door on the left side of the passageway. The floors were wood, not dirt as Kaya had envisioned in her log cabin fantasy. In front of her was a rectangular wooden table. It was already set with a clean white tablecloth and three deep dish plates and spoons. The hearth was in the middle of the opposite wall. A small bed of coals warmed the sturdy iron pot suspended there. Left of the hearth was a work table with various cooking utensils and pottery. To the right of the main door was a tall pine pie safe.

Two beds placed end-to-end occupied the far end of the room to her right. Each bore a colorful quilt. Curtains hung from the ceiling of that end of the cabin. They were pulled aside now but could be closed around each bed for privacy and warmth while sleeping.

Large glass-paned windows flanked the fireplace. Kaya had learned from her father that when building a home, if you placed windows in the south-facing walls, you could make the best use of natural light and save on candles and lamp oil. It was hard to tell now that it was dark outside, but Kaya was willing to bet this was the case in Olena's sensible Norwegian home. Another window was in the wall to her left, the front of the cabin. Kaya now understood how her grandmother could have seen their approach from her rocking chair or from the table, which would have given her plenty of time to set three places.

As her grandmother bustled about getting supper ready, Kaya had a chance to observe her without seeming rude. Olena Olson was of average height for a woman. She wore a plain black dress Kaya had come to expect from women of Olena's age. It fit her slim build, narrow at the waist and broadening into a wide skirt at her feet. She wore her dark hair parted in the middle, smooth on top and twisted into a no-nonsense bun at the nape of her neck. She moved about the cabin with little wasted motion. Olena Olson was clearly not ready for the rocking chair, even though one sat near the hearth.

Olena noticed Kaya watching her. "What is it, dear?"

The answer to an important question about her mother's death was standing right in front of her. "Nothing. It's just that . . ."

Olena smiled and waited for her to finish.

Kaya took a deep breath. "Well, how are you? That is, how are you feeling?"

"Aren't you sweet! Traveling for days, and the first thing you want to know is how I am feeling. I am feeling well as always, but so much better now that you and father are here, safe and sound."

"You haven't been sick?"

"Sick? Why, no, dear. Not in ages. Healthy as a horse. What makes you think that?"

So Tante Julia was right. Bestemor wasn't sick. She had her answer, but it just created more questions. Was Papa right – did she mis-hear or misunderstand about the destination of her mother's trip? Kaya didn't think so. If she *had* heard right, but *Bestemor* wasn't sick, why else was Mama headed to Preston?

Before she could answer her grandmother, Lars'

heavy steps clunked through the middle passage between the cabins. A few moments later he filled the door. "Think what?"

"Kaya thought I had been sick. Where on earth would she get an idea like that?"

Lars frowned at Kaya. "Kaya, I thought we agreed there's nothing more to say on that subject."

"Yes, sir."

Olena's eyebrows lifted at his tone.

Lars rubbed the back of his neck. "It's a long story, *Mor,* and it's been a long three days. " he said. "Can we talk about it later?"

"Oh. Of course." Olena looked from father to daughter and back again. "Well, don't just stand there," she said, gesturing them forward. "Sit down before you fall down. The stew is ready."

At the mention of supper, Kaya remembered something *Onkel* Otto had said. Since it was not on the topic of her grandmother's health, she thought it would be safe to mention. Kaya turned to her grandmother and asked as politely as she knew how, "Excuse me please, but what kind of stew?"

"Kaya!" Lars said.

"Lars, it's fine," Olena said. Turning to Kaya, she said, "My goodness, you're just full of questions, aren't you? Beef, of course. It's beef stew. I raise cattle. And hogs. Didn't you know? I raise sheep here too, but I raise them for their wool. Do you like beef stew?"

"Oh, yes ma'am!" Kaya answered.

"Otto was telling Kaya all about squirrel stew," Lars explained.

"Squirrel! We have plenty of beef and pork here on the ranch. We leave the squirrels alone." Olena dismissed the idea with a wave. "Squirrels are troll food. Any Norwegian worth their salt knows that."

Troll food - that's just what Mama used to say. More than the delicious smells, more than the cheery room, those familiar words warmed Kaya's heart.

Lars moved to the chair at the far end of the table and looked to his mother before sitting.

"Yes, sit at your usual place, son," Olena said. She gestured to another chair. "Go ahead and sit by your father, dear," she said to Kaya. "Even though I have been living alone for a while, I leave all of the chairs out for when visitors drop by. Now that you two are here, I am sure we will have plenty of visitors who want to see you

47

again, Lars, and meet Kaya." She turned to her granddaughter. "I suppose I should make a few extra pies tomorrow. Would you like to help me?"

"Yes, ma'am." Kaya's mother was not much of a cook, but Kaya had spent many afternoons in *Tante* Julia's kitchen. Everything she knew about kitchen chores, she had learned there.

Olena ladled the stew into all three plates, then took the chair to Lars' right and directly across from Kaya. "It's been a long time, son. Will you say grace?"

"Of course, *Mor*." The three bowed their heads over their meal as Lars said a few words.

> *I Jesu navn går vi til bords*
> *å spise, drikke på ditt ord.*
> *Deg, Gud til ære, oss til gavn,*
> *Så får vi mat i Jesu navn.*
>
> In Jesus' name to the table we go
> To eat and drink according to His word.
> To God the honor, us the gain,
> So we have food in Jesus' name.

"*Amen,*" they chorused.

Kaya picked up her spoon. Her mouth watered at

the delicious aroma of the beef and vegetables, but she knew better than to start before the adults. Her father tucked into the stew in earnest, ignoring everything else around him. Olena watched him fondly, then had a spoonful herself.

Kaya took that as her cue and tasted the stew. It was just the right temperature and did not disappoint. The beef was tender and flavorful. The carrots and potatoes were firm but not mushy. The broth was thick, and her grandmother had been generous with the salt. Kaya thought she would never taste any better cooking than *Tante* Julia's. *Bestemor* Olson had just proved her wrong.

Kaya admired the carved wooden spoon she had been using. "Look, Papa. These spoons are just like the ones you carved for us."

Lars nodded. "Yes, they are. My father – your *Bestefar* - carved those a long time ago. I learned to carve spoons from him when I was about your age."

"When will you teach me?"

"Carving is not for girls. You need to concentrate on your sewing and cooking."

"Nonsense," Olena said. "If all I did around here was the sewing and the cooking, how would the firewood get chopped? The cattle tended? The fall crops planted?" Olena winked at Kaya and took another bite of her stew. "How about your schooling, Kaya? Your Norwegian is perfect. How is your English?"

Kaya switched to English and said, "My teacher says it is very good. What do you think?"

Olena smiled approvingly and replied in English. "Your teacher is right. I see your parents have raised you well."

Kaya set down her spoon. She blinked rapidly but wasn't ready to look up from her lap yet.

Olena reached out and gave Kaya's hand a gentle squeeze. "I know this must be difficult for you, Kaya," she said softly. "We will take things one day at a time. Just know how happy I am to have you both here." Olena cleared her throat and changed the subject. "Would anyone like some more stew?"

"Thank you, *Mor*, that would be wonderful," Lars agreed hastily.

"My goodness, Lars. You eat as if you haven't had a decent meal in a week!" Olena said as she refilled her son's bowl. When she raised her eyebrows in silent question to Kaya, Kaya nodded for another helping as well.

"Even with a good wagon and strong horse, it still makes for a long trip from Normandy," said Lars. "It's always nice to have a hot meal."

"Don't tell me you didn't see anything worth shooting for lunch?" Olena asked. "There's plenty of game between here and Preston, and that's only a few miles away."

"I didn't want to waste any ammunition," Lars answered. He clamped his mouth shut as soon as the words were out, but out they were. Lars ducked his head and spooned stew into his mouth as if it were the last meal he would ever eat.

Olena stiffened in her chair. Kaya frowned at her sudden alertness, then followed her glance and looked to her father. "And why is that?" Olena asked.

Lars sighed and put down his spoon. "Just being prudent."

"In case of bandits. Or Indians," Kaya added.

"Indians? *Pffft.*" Olena waved a hand in dismissal.

"Maybe not *pffft*," Lars said, mimicking her wave. "Didn't anyone write you about the Foss boy?"

"Ole Foss's boy?" Olena asked. "No. What happened?"

"I am surprised you have not heard. Kaya, your grandmother is a walking newspaper. Nothing happens in this town, or maybe in the entire county, that she doesn't know about."

"I like to be well-informed," Olena said primly. "This must have slipped by me. What happened to the Foss boy?"

"Well-"

"Indians got him!" Kaya blurted.

Two sets of pale blue eyes turned in her direction. Lars sat back in his chair. "She is obsessed with this story," he explained to his mother. "Proceed," he said to Kaya, gesturing with one hand as if to pave the way for her.

"Please do," Olena said. "I cannot wait to hear it now." She smiled at Kaya to go ahead with the story.

"Ole was kidnapped," Kaya said, the words tumbling out. "Ole the boy, not Ole the father. They are both named Ole. Ole was out gathering firewood at the cedar break outside of Normandy. Indians came and took him away."

Olena sat back, shocked. "Is this true?" she asked Lars.

Lars nodded. "Comanches. Some townspeople went

after them, but they lost the trail after two days of hard riding."

Olena turned back to Kaya. "Did you know this boy well?"

"Not really," Kaya said. "He's older than me. He only came to my school when he wasn't working on his farm."

"How old is he? Is he too young to fight them off?"

Lars snorted. "If the Indians come for you, unless you are armed, you don't fight them off. Your best hope is that they want to keep you safe and sound to trade you later for liquor and guns. If you fight back and are too much trouble, they will kill you on the spot." Seeing the look on Kaya's face, he added, "Foss was a fool to send an unarmed boy out so far alone. It was unfortunate. But the chance of anything like that happening around here is unlikely."

Olena agreed. "I'm glad you two were traveling east instead of west. I read in the Dallas newspapers about all sorts of trouble they have closer to the frontier. But your *Bestefar* Olson, may he rest in peace, used to say there were far worse things here than Indians. And he was proved right."

Kaya said. "What is worse than Indians? Do you mean bandits?"

Lars sighed. He and his mother exchanged looks. "I'm sorry, son. It's been so long since I had to remember to hold my tongue around children. But she's hardly a child anymore."

"I suppose she had to find out sooner or later," Lars said.

"Find out what?" Kaya asked, bursting with curiosity.

Olena gathered her thoughts. "Your *Bestefar* Olson, my Andreas, was a good man, an honest man. . ." She paused, then began again. "Kaya, times were hard here during the war. Maybe it was the same in Normandy?"

"Yes, ma'am. When Papa came back from fighting, he said it was hard to find a job that would pay in real money. He said too many people were coming west because of the war. And Mama was mad because there wasn't any fabric, or coffee."

"Yes, no coffee! I hope to never again drink coffee made from chicory, or corn meal, or okra seeds . . ." Seeing Kaya's nose wrinkled in distaste, Olena said, "Oh yes – roasted okra seeds! Coffee, sugar, cotton, jobs, and lots of other things were hard to get. Money was scarce. Even if we had money, there wasn't much to buy. Between the Galveston blockade and our men off fighting the war, there was no way to get the things we needed, no one to plant and harvest the crops. But we survived." Olena enjoyed a sip of her real coffee. "So many men went to fight. Many of them didn't come back. Most Texans fought for the South, but some didn't. Our local men, Norwegian men, fought for the South, even though most thought slavery was wrong."

"Then why did they fight for the South?"

"It was a hard decision. But when you are new to an area, like we were, it was important to get along with your new neighbors. Being anti-slavery was not popular here, even dangerous."

"So *Bestefar* Olson died in the war?" Kaya asked. "I thought Papa's brother was the one who got killed."

"They are both gone now, Kaya. You are right about your *Onkel* Neil. He died at Pleasant Hill. But my Andreas – Andreas came home to me safe and sound from the war. Last year – June 8th to be exact – he went to town to pick up the mail. Three men rode into town with bandanas over their faces-"

"Bandits!" Kaya breathed.

"They must have been looking for him, because when he came out of the Preston Hotel, one of the men shot him, right there in broad daylight. The three of them were gone before my poor Andreas was dead."

Kaya leaned forward, shocked. "In town? In the daytime? Who did it, *Bestemor*?"

"We don't know, Kaya. Sheriff Bradley did his best. He is a good man, but he didn't get much cooperation." Olena sighed and patted Kaya's leg. "So now you know, Kaya. Your *Bestefar* was murdered. Some people think it was a random act, you know – some toughs passing through, running from the war. But I will always believe it was someone who knew exactly what they were doing. I believe my Andreas was murdered because he was against slavery, like most other Norwegians."

Kaya sat silently, taking in this information about *Bestefar* Olson. As she peered past her grandmother's shoulder, a dark shape appeared and scraped against the glass. Kaya pushed away from the table and gasped. Lars and Olena jerked toward the window in alarm. Then the shape barked.

"Odin!" Lars said. "I forgot all about you, boy.

Where have you been?" He went to the pot over the hearth and fished around inside with a long handled spoon.

"Who on earth is Odin?" Olena asked, recovering from the start.

"He's our dog," Kaya said. "He's the best dog in the world. He helps Papa hunt, and he barks when strangers come around."

"Dog? I didn't see him when you arrived. I hope he doesn't like sheep," Olena said. "We will have to make sure he doesn't get a taste for them."

"Don't worry, *Mor*," Lars said. "We got Odin from an American who raises sheep. Odin is used to them. He knows he's not supposed to eat them." At last he brought up a bone from the bottom of the soup pot. "Do you mind?"

Olena waved her approval. Lars grabbed the warm bone with a dish cloth and headed outside.

"Well, I must say I like his name," Olena said to Kaya. "Is he much like the other Odin?"

"What other Odin?" Kaya asked.

Olena smiled. "When your father was a boy, he had a dog named Odin. They went everywhere together. I can't believe he hasn't told you about Odin the First."

"*Mor*," Lars sighed, returning to his seat at the table. "if you're going to start telling tales, I'm going to start unloading the wagon." With that, he turned back around and headed outside.

Olena laughed and said to Kaya, "Good. Now I can tell you some stories and he won't be here to shush me."

"What stories, *Bestemor*?" Kaya asked. She brought their bowls to the work table while her grandmother poured some water into a large washtub. They fell into the familiar routine of washing and drying the dishes.

"Well, my favorite story about Lars and Odin is the time Lars and his brother, your *Onkel* Neil, were out hunting rabbits with Odin."

"*Onkel* Neil – the one who died in the war?"

Olena nodded. "Yes, dear. May he rest in peace. Neil and your father, they lost sight of the rabbit. Lars passed an old hollow log and felt sure the rabbit had hidden inside. He reached into the log to feel around for the rabbit, and snap! Something bit him. He pulled his hand out of the log and a big rat was attached, his teeth sunken in right here." She wiped her hands on her apron and pointed to the tender spot between her thumb and index finger.

"A rat! Ugh!" Kaya dried the last of the bowls and

58

set it with the other bowls on the corner sideboard.

"Yes, and it was not about to let go without a fight. That's how rats are, you know. Lars shook that rat as hard as he could until finally it came loose. Quick as a flash, Odin the First snatched the rat out of the air before it hit the ground and crushed it in his jaws."

"*That's* why Papa hates rats so much," Kaya said.

"Oh yes, he surely does."

"Do you have any more stories, *Bestemor*?"

Olena nodded. "Yes, child, many more. But I will save them for another time. Thanks to your help, that's the last of the dishes. Let's go have a look at your new home."

Listening to her grandmother's tales, she had almost forgotten about the other half of the house. Kaya followed her out the door and into the other half of the dwelling.

"It's like yours, only backwards," Kaya said. The hearth was in the middle of opposite wall, windows on either side. Once Lars moved their table, chairs and beds inside, the two cabins would be quite similar.

"Here's the bedding," Lars puffed as he dragged two mattresses through the door. "They are soft enough to sleep on the floor tonight. I'll set up the beds tomorrow."

Olena nodded. "You two must be exhausted. Kaya,

why don't you sleep in my spare bed tonight? We can get you two settled in tomorrow. I am sure your father won't mind sleeping in here by himself."

Kaya compared the comfortable room next door to this dark, empty space. "May I, Papa?" Kaya asked. Lars gave a quick nod.

"Good, that's settled for tonight anyway. I'll make some coffee for us, and Kaya can go to bed."

They returned to Olena's side of the cabin. "Kaya, you can sleep right here." She indicated one of the two beds at the far end of the room. "We will try not to make too much noise."

Kaya couldn't imagine either of them making any noise at all. Then she saw from her grandmother's twinkle that she was teasing. Already Kaya was looking forward to getting to know her better.

After she changed into her sleeping clothes, Kaya got into bed and pulled the brightly patterned curtain closed. The space was dark and cozy and she snuggled in. So much had happened today. Tomorrow she would help her grandmother bake pies and set up their new home next door. Maybe she would hear some more stories. Visitors might come. The knot of sadness she had been carrying inside her loosened.

Kaya awoke out of a deep sleep into an unfamiliar dark. This wasn't her bed, or her room. As she lay getting her bearings, she recognized her father's low rumble. Then she remembered where she was, in *Bestemor* Olson's cabin. Papa and *Bestemor* were still talking. Kaya turned over and tried to go back to sleep. But the only thing between her and the rest of the cabin was a thin layer of calico. Was it still eavesdropping if you couldn't help it? She thought about making a noise to let them know she was awake. As she thought about what to do, she strained to listen in spite of herself.

"Why didn't you tell me sooner?"

"Lars, what good would it have done? You had a wife and a child to think about. It was best for everyone to let it be."

"But Jesse Spence? Anyone but him!"

"I'm sorry, son. At least you won't have to worry about running into him. He's disappeared again, as usual."

"How long has he been gone?"

"Two, three weeks, I suppose. Why?"

"That's around when Alma died. Did you know she

claimed she was coming to visit you? She said you were sick."

"So that's why Kaya asked after my health. How is she taking all this?"

"As well as could be expected. She thinks it's her fault."

Their voices lowered, their words becoming indistinct. But the questions chattered on in her mind. *Who is this Spence person? Why was her father so agitated? What did it have to do with her mother?* Kaya feared leaving Normandy also meant leaving behind the answers about her mother's death. It seemed the move to Preston created new questions. If the answers were also in Preston, she meant to find them.

CHAPTER FIVE

After a few days at her grandmother's home, Kaya was settling into a new routine. As in Normandy, there was much to do. Unlike there, much more of the work at her new home was outdoors.

In Normandy, Kaya helped with the cooking and cleaning when she wasn't in school. She had inherited her mother's dislike of cooking, so she became expert at washing dishes to avoid cooking chores whenever possible. Even the drudgery of making soap in the fall was preferable to drying *lutefisk* and peeling potatoes for *lefse*.

One household task Kaya's mother had enjoyed was needlework. She made all of the Olson family's clothes, except for Lars' work pants - they were too heavy to sew by hand. Alma Olson also sewed for other Norwegians in the community. They brought her dresses to be repaired or re-styled, giving tired old dresses a new look. Kaya learned how to sew from her mother, although she didn't particularly care for the activity. Alma was often impatient with the quality of Kaya's stitches and numerous pricked fingers.

At the Olson ranch, much to her relief, Kaya had little time for sewing. As promised, she helped her grandmother bake some peach pies the day after they arrived. Kaya enjoyed it more than she thought she would. Unlike Kaya's mother, her grandmother clearly had a knack for cooking. Her enthusiasm was contagious. Kaya also helped with the dishes and the housework. But there was much more to be done outdoors. Olena's cabin was not much bigger than Kaya's home in Normandy, but the property around it stretched out of sight. "Over six hundred acres," Olena had told her. There were scores of cattle, a large flock of sheep, hundreds of hogs roaming freely, and wild turkeys.

Olena and a hired man named John Whitney did most of the work. After the war, John and thousands of slaves like him were freed by their former masters. But they had few possessions and no resources. Many became sharecroppers, or renters, on someone else's land. In John's case, he had an agreement with Olena. Olena had plenty of land but no one to help her manage it. John was willing to work hard, but had no land. So in return for half of what he produced, Olena agreed to allow John to farm some of her land. She provided the tools, seeds, work animals, and a home. He lived on the far west side of the Olson property in a snug log cabin with his wife, Zelphia, and two young sons.

John worked hard. But there were still plenty of chores for Olena, and now Kaya, to do. First thing in the morning, they collected eggs from the hen house. Olena showed her how to reach under the nesting hens without disturbing them. "We have plenty of eggs," Olena told her. "I usually take the extras over to John. But we will still have enough for the three of us."

Cows were milked twice daily. At first, Kaya was wary of the stocky beasts. As she sat on the milking stool, they towered far above her head. But she soon found they were quite gentle. She had to lean in to reach their udders, and they let her rest her cheek on their sleek brown sides as she milked. They didn't seem to mind her inexperienced tugging on their udders to squirt the milk into a metal pail below. Except for Bella. Bella was an older cow. She snorted and switched her tail if Kaya did not get the milk flowing right away.

Kaya also gathered kindling for the hot water wash on Monday, which was laundry day. Olena paid Zelphia Whitney to help with the laundry. Zelphia was friendly to Kaya and patiently answered her questions about scrub boards and irons and wringers. Kaya was thankful laundry day was only once a week. After a long day of hauling the sopping wet clothes from wash to rinse to wringer to clothes line, Kaya awoke the next day to find she had fallen asleep before she had a chance to eat supper.

Perhaps the biggest adjustment so far was how often she was left to fend for herself. In Normandy, Kaya was rarely alone. At home or at school or at church, people were always nearby. The Olson cabin was far from the nearest neighbor, and even farther from town. Kaya's grandmother, father, and the Whitneys were the only people she had seen there so far. It was a large operation. They had many tasks to attend to. Her grandmother explained the day's activities, then expected Kaya to handle herself on her own.

Today Kaya knelt in the neat rows of her grandmother's garden. The earth was dry from the Texas summer heat. Dirt clods poked her knees through her homespun dress. Tending the sprawling plot could easily keep Kaya busy until school started in the fall. She worked her way up and down the long rows, plucking out a struggling weed here and there among the carrots, peas and beans. There was far more food than her grandmother and the Whitneys could eat, so Olena sold the excess.

The merciless Texas sun beat down on Kaya. She wiped her face on her sleeve and headed inside, looking for her bonnet. While her eyes adjusted to the darker interior she scanned their side of the cabin, hands on her hips. Her eyes alighted on her mother's trunk. There were sure to be one or two bonnets inside. Although they may be a little big for her, they would be better than no bonnet at all.

Kaya pried the leather straps loose and opened the trunk. Everything lay just as it was when she buckled it closed before they left Normandy.

On top was her mother's second-favorite dress, a green wool that flattered her fair hair and complexion. Her favorite blue dress, the same color as her eyes, was the one *Tante* Julia had chosen for the burial. Kaya lifted the green dress carefully. Below it was her mother's *bunad*, the dress she wore for her wedding and other special Norwegian holidays. With its high waist and lace bodice, it was quite different from the American-style green wool. Stored below the dresses were plain white undergarments, a few lace collars, a hairbrush and mirror. Under these lay two quilt tops awaiting batting and backing, and her travel satchel. As Kaya's fingers pushed toward the bottom of the trunk, they encountered something small and hard. She took firmer hold of it and gently pulled it out. It was her mother's carved wooden dala horse.

Its once pristine white paint was now faded in some places, but delicate curving flowers of orange and blue still adorned the horse's back. Kaya traced the arch of its broad neck. This little horse was one of her mother's favorite possessions. "My sweetheart made it for me," was all she had said, when Kaya asked where she got it.

"Kaya?"

Kaya jumped. She dropped the carved horse into her apron pocket. "Yes, Papa?"

"How would you like to take a break from your gardening? I need to ride into town to talk to Mr. Jensen about the school we are building. Your grandmother is coming, too. She wants to stop at the general store. We thought you would like to come with us."

"Yes, sir, I surely would!" Town! Kaya enjoyed helping her grandmother on the ranch, but she missed the bustle of Normandy. She dashed out to the cistern, blonde pigtails flying. She took a quick drink and washed her hands. Olena Olson was already in the wagon waiting for them. Kaya climbed into the back.

"How far is Preston, *Bestemor*?" she asked, a little out of breath.

"Not far. About three miles." She fanned herself briefly. "I sometimes walk if the weather is nice and I don't have too many parcels to bring back."

The wagon tilted and creaked as Lars climbed aboard. He clicked to Old Ned and they turned around in the yard. Odin cocked one eyebrow as he dozed under the oak tree. "Stay here, boy," Lars said, and Odin returned to his nap without objection.

Kaya leaned against the back of the wagon seat and listened to her father and grandmother discuss the price of wheat, whether it might rain any time soon, and how much the cotton crops might bring this year. She soon lost interest in their conversation and watched the countryside pass by from her backwards perspective. The prairie grass lay surrendered to the late summer heat, wilted and dull. Heat mirages shimmered in the distance. Two buzzards circled in the cloudless sky. *Something dead there.*

The clip-clop of horse shoes on hardpack got Kaya's attention. Two riders approached from the direction of Preston. As they drew near, the riders slowed and her father did the same.

"Howdy, Miz Olson." The older of the two men tipped his hat. A dull badge peeked from beneath his leather vest.

"Morning, Sheriff Bradley. You remember my son, Lars?"

"Lars Olson!" The sheriff exclaimed, extending a hand. "You were a young sprout last I saw you. Don't you live in Normandy?"

Lars started to answer, but his mother beat him to it. "Lars lost his wife, Bill. He and Kaya live with me now."

The sheriff's sharp eyes picked out Kaya in the back of the wagon. "Sorry for your loss, Lars. My sympathies to you."

Lars nodded in thanks.

"We're on our way into town for a few supplies," Olena said. "What about you and young Sammy here? You look like you are on official business."

"We are, I'm afraid." Sheriff Bradley removed his hat, wiped his forehead with his forearm, then put his hat back on. "I'm glad I ran into you out here. There was some trouble outside of Tyler. One of their freight wagons never made it to Preston. It's been missing going on a couple weeks now."

"Freight wagon?" Olena asked. "Not Elijah Granger's outfit?"

The sheriff nodded. "Yes'm, I'm afraid so. We're not sure, but we think it might have been robbed. We're on our way out there to talk to their sheriff and see if trouble might be headed our way. You be sure to keep your eyes open out at your place. Let me know if you see any strangers passing through in a hurry." He glanced at Lars. "It's good that you have a man around the house again, Miz Olson. These are hard times." He touched his hat again. The younger man, Sammy, did likewise, and they rode away at a steady clip.

"Well, that's a real shame," Olena said.

"Do you know this man, Granger?" Lars asked.

"Know of him. His folks have a dry goods store in Tyler. He served in the war with your brother."

"Bandits!" Kaya exhaled.

"Now Kaya," Lars began. "It's nothing to worry about. No bandits are interested in an empty wagon."

71

Soon they approached the town of Preston and Kaya relaxed a little. Surely bandits would not attack in town in broad daylight! Then she remembered what happened to her *Bestefar*. She was glad for the rifle her father had retrieved from the footboard. It now lay across his lap. Kaya couldn't help but think their wagon wouldn't be empty on their way home.

CHAPTER SIX

People of all ages, shapes and sizes strolled along Preston's wide main street. Kaya could see two hotels and a general store from where she sat. A blacksmith's efforts banging hammer to anvil rang out nearby. Two horses grazed on a pile of hay in a corral at the end of the street. The town jail sat wedged between one of the hotels and a saddle shop. Wagons loaded with cotton bales lined up to enter a large building one block back. Horses and wagons passed in both directions. Many of those passing by called out a greeting to Olena Olson.

"*Bestemor*, do you know everyone in Preston?" Kaya asked.

Her grandmother smiled. "I might, at that."

Lars stopped the wagon in front of a large general store. "Is it always this busy?" he asked his mother.

"Well, it is Thursday. The stage comes on Monday, Thursday, and Saturday so it is pretty lively on those days."

"Mr. Jensen said to meet him at his store," Lars said. "You two go ahead to Bakken's and I will meet you there when I am finished." He helped them out of the wagon, then climbed back up and headed down the street. A sign above one of the buildings there said "Jens Jensen, Druggist".

"What's 'Bakken's', *Bestemor*?" Kaya asked as she stood taking it all in.

"It's one of the two general stores in Preston," Olena said, gesturing toward the store directly across the street. "I like doing business with Mr. Bakken. We came here from Norway on the same ship. We have been friends for many years."

After waiting for a lull in traffic, Olena and Kaya crossed the dusty street and entered the general store.

"*God morgen*, Olena!" called a voice from inside the store.

"*Hei*, Carl," she answered. "I would like you to meet my granddaughter, Kaya. Kaya, this is Mr. Bakken."

Kaya did a quick curtsy. Mr. Bakken was the same height as her grandmother. What was left of his snow-white hair fringed around his head, leaving the top bald and shining. His build was round and ample. Kaya imagined if she poked his tummy, he would feel like a new down pillow.

"So this is Kaya," Mr. Bakken said. His blue eyes smiled when his mouth did. Kaya could not help but smile back. "*God dag*," he said with a formal bow. "I was sorry to hear about your mother."

"*Mange takk*," Kaya replied.

"What lovely manners," Mr. Bakken said to Olena.

Kaya blushed.

Olena said, "Kaya, I need to talk to Mr. Bakken about our shopping list. Take a look around if you like. I'll just be a minute." Olena and Mr. Bakken headed to the rear of the store.

Kaya took a few steps further into the store. It was similar to the general store in Normandy, only bigger. The wooden floors creaked beneath her feet. The store smelled of fresh sawdust, leather, and new fabric. Light filtered in through the windows along the front wall. Shelves covered the other three walls from floor to ceiling. Groceries, household goods, and kitchen wares were on the right side of the store running the entire length of that wall. A long glass-fronted counter on the left side contained smaller items such as toys, candies, and at the farthest end, guns. At the rear of the store bolts of fabric filled the shelves. Kaya could make out a few hats, shoes and boots back there as well. People milled about, placing orders with the clerks, examining the merchandise, or, like Kaya, just browsing.

Kaya turned to the glass counter to inspect the penny candy. In the next case lay a generous selection of knives. They were laid out on a background of crimson felt from longest to shortest.

"Those Bowie knives are fancy, but the Barlows fit in your pocket," a voice said. "They're nice, but my pa's are better." A boy not quite her size stood next to her at the counter. A lion's mane of wavy light brown hair framed his face. His smile revealed a gap from a missing tooth. "My name's Zach. You're a Norskie, aren't you? I heard you talking Norskie to Mr. Bakken. I sure hope you know English cause I sure can't talk Norskie. Are you new in town? Do you know Miz Olson? My ma knows Miz Olson. Everybody knows Miz Olson. Everybody knows my ma cause she's the schoolteacher. Everybody knows everybody in this town. Everybody 'cept you. Hey, whatsamatter? Can't you talk? I bet you can't even talk any English. My pa says you people shouldn't come over here if you don't want to learn to talk English. He says you should go back to where you came from. I guess you Norskies are all alike."

Kaya stared at Zach in astonishment. "*Speak* English."

It was Zach's turn to be astonished. "What'd you say?"

"It's *speak* English, not *talk* English. I can speak English, same as you."

"She's right, Zach."

Kaya turned to see who was agreeing with her. A woman stood behind her, smiling. She was about Kaya's mother's age, but they could not have been more different. Alma Olson had been small in stature. She was curvy, but not yet plump like *Tante* Julia (although it would not be hard to imagine her that way some day). Kaya had inherited Alma's thick, wavy blonde hair. The newcomer, in contrast, was nearly as tall as Kaya's father. Her plain gray dress fit her slender form perfectly. The bonnet hanging loosely down her back revealed hair so black it was almost blue. Eyes the color of summer grass gazed out of a complexion creamy as that morning's milk.

"Hello," the woman said, smiling. "I'm Zachary's mother. You'll have to excuse him. You would think a teacher's son would know his grammar rules, but sometimes he gets in a hurry. Zach, who's your new friend?"

"I don't know, Ma. She didn't tell me yet."

Footsteps approached from behind Zach and his mother.

"Kaya?"

The beautiful woman turned around at the sound of Lars' voice. Her father stopped dead in his tracks. He gaped at Zach's mother, opening and closing his mouth. Kaya felt the air around them change. It seemed thicker, like before a spring thunderstorm. Finally, the woman said the one thing Kaya did not expect: "Hello, Lars."

"Hello, Lucy." Lars removed his hat and nodded once, quickly. A few moments of silence passed, then both spoke at once.

"I didn't know-"

"It's good to-"

"Sorry." Lars gestured with his hat for Lucy to continue.

"I didn't know you were in town. Are you visiting

your mother?"

"Yes, well. . ."

"We live here now," Kaya volunteered. Both adults turned to look at her.

"Live here?"

"Alma passed away, Lucy," explained Lars in smooth, nearly unaccented English. "We are living with Mother until we get settled." Kaya gaped at him. She couldn't remember the last time she heard her father speak English. She had almost forgotten he knew how.

"How awful, Lars. I'm so sorry." Lucy stood there, her hand at her throat. She glanced at Kaya again. "So this is . . . "

"This is Kaya. Kaya, this is Miss Carlisle . . . "

"Mrs. Spence now, Lars."

"Yes, of course. Spence. I just heard about that. Of course you would have married by now," Lars babbled. "Kaya, this is Mrs. Spence."

Spence? That's the name Bestemor and Papa mentioned last night. Kaya eyed the pretty woman with renewed interest.

Zach had been watching the entire exchange from behind his mother's skirts. Unable to hold back any longer, he stepped up and tugged at her hand.

"Oh yes, and this is my son Zachary. Zach, this is Mr. Olson. And the mystery is solved about your new friend here."

"You know him?" Zach nodded toward Lars.

"Yes, son," Mrs. Lucy Carlisle Spence smiled. "I know him."

Olena returned from the rear of the store to find quite a gathering at the knife counter. "Hello, Lars. Finished already? My goodness - Lucy, and little Zachary. What a pleasant surprise."

"Hello, Olena," Lucy said. "I was just telling Lars I was so sorry to hear about Alma."

"Thank you, dear."

The small group stood awkwardly, each waiting for someone else to speak. Lars' eyes never left Lucy Spence. Lucy glanced away first, pretending to pick a non-existent thread from her skirt. Her perfect skin flushed a delicate pink. Olena watched the two of them, repressing a smile. Kaya's eyes darted from face to face to face, tracking the complex signals ricocheting among the adults above. Finally, Lars cleared his throat. "We should be going, Mother. I want to get the supplies home and unloaded."

"Yes, yes, of course. Go ahead and bring the wagon around back. Carl has my order waiting. He has everything but the quinine. Did Jensen's have any?"

Lars shook his head 'no'. "It was on the freight wagon that was robbed, so he won't have any until next week."

"There was a robbery?" Lucy asked.

"It seems so," Olena said. "We saw Sheriff Bradley on our way into town. He and Sam were headed to Tyler to see about it."

The pink drained out of Lucy Spence's cheeks. Lars and Olena exchanged a look. "Something wrong, Lucy?" Olena asked.

Lucy blinked. "No, no," she said. "Nothing wrong."

"Well then . . ." Lars said. When no one else spoke, he lifted his hat to the group and disappeared out the rear of the store.

"You must be delighted to have him home again," Lucy said, watching Lars as he left.

"Oh yes, delighted to have them both," answered Olena. "I am sure you will be seeing more of Kaya once the new school is built."

Lucy glanced at Kaya. "Olena, there's a camp

meeting setting up at Four Mile Prairie. We're going on Saturday night. Why don't you come and bring Kaya? She and Zach are about the same age. They could get to know each other and she could meet some of the other children before school starts."

"Camp meeting?" Olena said. "I don't know. Let me think about it. If we decide to come, I will be sure to find you there."

"Fair enough," said Lucy. "Come along, Zach. We need to be going. Goodbye, Olena. Nice meeting you, Kaya. Welcome to Preston."

"Thank you," Kaya answered. As they left, Zach twisted around to look at Kaya until he was out of the building.

"I suppose we better go out back to make sure your father loaded the right order," Olena said. Kaya smiled to think of her father making a mistake like that. Now she *knew* her grandmother was having a little joke. Kaya followed Olena to the rear of the store. They stepped out into the bright sunshine and watched Lars load the sacks of flour, sugar and other supplies into the wagon.

"*Bestemor*, what's a camp meeting?"

"A camp meeting is a type of church service. In

Norway it was hard to find a church that was not Lutheran. But here in America, there are so many different kinds, I can't name them all. We have our Lutheran church, of course. There are the Baptists, and the Methodists, and-"

"The Catholics?" Kaya offered.

"Yes, of course, the Catholics, too. Not all of these churches have buildings like our church here in Preston. Rather than have people come to a building on Sunday to worship, sometimes the preacher travels to places where no church is available and has the service outside. I hear they can go on for days. I have always wondered what they are like. Would you like to go?"

"Are they Lutherans?"

"Oh no, dear. Far from it."

"I don't know if Papa would let me."

"If you want to come with me, I will speak to him about it." A small gang of children ran down the street. They shouted and laughed as one of them did his best to push a metal barrel hoop before him with a forked tree limb. "Kaya, did you know many American children in Normandy?"

Kaya watched the children as they disappeared around the corner of Mr. Bakken's store. "Not many.

Mama sent me to school at the Norwegian church. All the kids there were Norskies – I mean, Norwegian."

"I'm sure you miss your friends."

"Not really. Mama said people you think are your friends will let you down, and that you have to be your own best friend."

Olena frowned. "But surely you had some friends your own age, children from school . . ." When Kaya didn't answer, Olena continued. "There aren't many Norwegian families in Preston anymore. Many of them moved to Normandy after the fever hit us hard during our first few years here. Normandy is a healthier place, they say. But there are plenty of American children in Preston. I'm sure you'll make some friends here."

Kaya shrugged. "*Bestemor*?"

"Yes?"

"How did that lady . . ."

"Mrs. Spence?"

"Yes, how did Mrs. Spence know Papa's name?"

"Why, they grew up together here. Lucy – Mrs. Spence – is only a year younger than your father."

"She's beautiful."

"Yes, she is.

Lars called over to them. "All finished, *Mor*. Are you two ready to head home?"

"Yes, indeed. Thank you so much for your help today, Lars. It makes such a difference to an old woman to have help with the heavy work."

"Now, *Mor*. You aren't an old woman quite yet." Lars helped his mother up onto the wagon seat. "Kaya, I left you a spot here among the flour sacks. It should be a more comfortable ride home than it was on the way over."

Kaya clambered into the bed of the wagon and found a cozy spot for herself among the sacks, crates and baskets of merchandise. Lars steered the wagon to the end of the buildings and back onto Preston's main street. A stage coach approached as they headed out of town.

Olena said, "It's about time! I was hoping the mail would arrive while we were here. Lars, stop for a minute while I see if I have any mail." Lars did as she asked and helped her down. She gathered her skirts and strode back down the street toward the stage coach.

The stage stopped in front of one of the hotels. The driver climbed down with a large set of saddlebags across one shoulder. He stopped to open the stage coach door and two men and a woman emerged. A piercing wail filled the air. Kaya covered her ears.

"That's the stage whistle," Lars explained when it ended a few moments later. "Henry over at the Preston Hotel blows it whenever the stage comes in so people will know the mail is here. And of course, everyone in town wants to know who arrived on the stage, or who will be leaving on it."

Kaya eyed the stage coach. "Papa," she said, "our wagon isn't empty anymore."

"What?"

"You said the bandits wouldn't bother us because our wagon was empty."

Lars turned around. "Kaya, there's nothing to fear. Do you think I would bring you and your grandmother with me if I thought anything might happen?"

"Well, no, but -"

"Kaya, sometimes bad things happen in this world. But you cannot go through life being afraid. The best you can do is remain alert and avoid foolish choices. That is all any of us can do."

Soon Olena returned with her mail. "My newspapers came," she said, waving them in the air. Lars hopped down and helped her back into her seat. Kaya turned around and knelt on one of the flour sacks so she could see what her grandmother had received.

"I am so happy to have regular mail service again," Olena said. "During the war, nothing came in. And the letters I tried to send never arrived."

She flipped through the papers as the wagon lurched forward. "Here is the *Herald* from Dallas. Oh, and *Norden* from Chicago. That one's in Norwegian," she explained. "Now we can see what's going on in the rest of the world."

CHAPTER SEVEN

Saturday morning found Kaya and Olena sitting in the shade of the cabin's front porch, churning butter from fresh milk. Kaya's arms ached from churning – up and down, up and down. She wiped her hands on her apron and lifted the lid of the churn. Large yellowish chunks floated on the surface of the milk inside. "Finally!" she said.

Olena laughed. "It is hard work, but worth it. There is nothing better than fresh butter on warm bread. I had a wonderful German girl to help me, the one who lived in your side of the cabin before you came. She got a letter from her brother in New Orleans and left to live with him. Delightful girl. Hard worker. She could milk the cows in half the time it takes us. Bertha was her name." Olena inspected the contents of the churn. "You're right. I think it's time for the butter to go into the mold."

The older woman showed Kaya how to use a slotted spoon to skim the butter out of the churn. Kaya packed the butter into a small crock and poured the remaining milk into another container. "There's a second bucket out by the well, Kaya," Olena said. "Lower the butter and the buttermilk into the well in the bucket so they will stay cool."

The wheel attached to the beam above the well squeaked as the rope slid through and the bucket disappear below. Kaya tied off the rope to keep the bucket far above water level.

Somewhere on the far side of the cabin, Odin began barking. "I had forgotten how handy it is to have a dog around," Olena said. "What on earth could that be about?"

"I don't know, but that's not Odin's angry bark," Kaya said.

"Not his angry bark?" Olena asked. "Pray tell, which bark is it?"

"I guess you could say it's his 'come look at this' bark. He's telling us there is something we should know about."

Olena peered into the distance and smiled. "Would you like to go investigate?" Olena asked on her way into the house. "I am sure it will be more interesting than all this talk of butter."

Kaya looked too, but didn't see anything. She headed toward Odin's barks. He was standing under large oak tree near the barn, staring toward the open prairie.

"What is it, boy?" Kaya said.

Odin barked once more. Then he wagged his tail madly back and forth. Kaya squinted into the distance and saw a small figure approaching. It was the boy from Bakken's.

"Hey, Norskie!"

"Zach," she said. "Where did you come from?"

"We live over there," he said, pointing behind himself. "Barely far enough to stretch my legs. My ma said you might like some company."

Kaya was glad to take a break from churning. But she wasn't sure she wanted to spend it with this American boy.

Odin dashed to greet Zach. The boy knelt and got a good face licking. "I wondered if you would set your dog on me," he said, scratching behind Odin's ears.

"I might, if you keep calling me Norskie."

"Oh. Sorry. Listen, I said some dumb stuff at the store yesterday. Sorry about that, too, Kaya." Odin nudged Zach's hand with his nose to encourage him to continue scratching, which he did.

"He's usually not so friendly with strangers," Kaya said. "If Odin thinks you're all right, I guess you're all right."

"Course I'm all right. Dogs know. They love me. What's his name?"

"Odin."

"Odin? What kind of a name is that?"

"It's Norwegian," Kaya said. "Odin was a powerful god in the old stories. We named him Odin because they are both good hunters."

"That's always handy, to have a good huntin' dog," Zach said. He looked around as he stood back up. The horses nibbled at the grass sprouting around the fence posts of the nearby corral. "Nice sorrel. Is she yours?"

"Sort of," Kaya said. "That's Dala. She was my mother's horse."

"Lucky! I wish I had a horse. Ma says maybe some day soon. Do you ride her?"

"I used to, but not since Mama died."

"Oh. Sorry." Zach's ears turned red. He scuffed a dirt clod with the toe of his shoe.

"Want to feed her?" Kaya asked. "*Bestemor* gave

me some carrots from the root cellar for the horses.

"Sure. Besta-what?"

"*Bestemor*. My grandmother." Kaya gestured toward the barn and they went inside. After retrieving some carrots from a basket in the tack area, they entered the corral. Kaya fed her carrot to Old Ned, and let Zach feed his to Dala. Both horses appreciated the treat, but when they realized no more carrots were forthcoming, resumed their foraging.

Odin started barking again. His nose and ears twitched madly in the direction Zach had come.

"Sic 'em, Odin," Zach urged. Odin glanced at Zach when he heard his name. He kept barking but did not move.

"Odin, *gå!*" Kaya said, pointing sharply toward the woods. Odin sped away. "His English is not very good," Kaya explained.

"Your dog speaks Norskie? Well, I guess that makes sense. Let's go see what he's after!" Zach said, and darted away.

Kaya turned back to look for her grandmother, but Olena was nowhere in sight. If she waited to run in and ask permission, Zach would be long gone. Hoping she was making the right choice, Kaya ran after him.

The children trailed Odin as he zig-zagged across the prairie in the mid-morning sun. They soon left the Olson cabin far behind. Odin tracked the scent, leaping over a narrow creek before stopping to focus his attention on a burrow near a large felled tree.

Zach and Kaya stood panting as Odin investigated his find. The dog dug madly, dirt spraying out between his hind legs. "Looks like we can rest for a minute," Zach said. "Once they get to digging, they're usually at it for a while."

Kaya nodded. "Zach, what's that over there?"

A stand of live oaks cast their shade over a patch of prairie the size of the corral at the Olson cabin. Zach peered into the shadows. "Oh. That's the old Striker cemetery. Not even a cemetery, really. Just a few graves for a family that used to live here."

Kaya was intrigued. "Out here in the middle of nowhere?"

"Yep."

"Can we go look at them?"

Zach shrugged.

"What's wrong, Zach? Scared?" Kaya teased.

"Heck no. I just don't like cemeteries, that's all."
Zach stomped off toward the pale gravestones. Kaya
trailed after him, Odin at her heels.

Thick underbrush hindered their approach. Odin
darted into the brush again, leaving the two children alone.
Briars tugged at Kaya's dress and one scratched her bare
arm. The live oak's leathery leaves filtered most of the
sunlight and muffled their footsteps. Even the birdsong was
quieter here. As they neared, more gravestones became
visible.

"These are all from the same family?" Kaya asked
quietly.

Zach nodded.

"So many . . ." she said. She walked between two
rows of gravestones. Some were tall, up to her knees. They
had various amounts of information carved into white
marble. Others were little more than large rocks marking
the head and foot of a grave. Crouching at the nearest one,
she brushed at some of the black lichen growing on its
carving and read the inscription aloud. "Samuel Striker,
born October 1, 1827, died May 25, 1852". Kaya turned to
the stone next to it. "Isaac Striker, 1845 to 1847, Angel."
She stood and counted the stones. "June 1852, another

June, July, October – what happened in 1852?"

"Fever. My ma said lots of folks got the fever and couldn't get the medicine they needed. Sometimes that happens around here."

"Fever? How do you get it?"

Zach shrugged. "I don't know. But I don't want it. Grandpa Carlisle had it and it was awful. He threw up blood."

Kaya made a face. "Seven graves," she said. "Do you think they all had the fever?"

"Maybe," Zach said. "And that's just the ones you can see. My ma says there are some that aren't marked."

"If they're not marked, how do you know they're here?"

"See that sunken spot over there? That's one. The ground sags a little sometimes when there has been some digging."

Kaya peered more closely at the ground around them. She soon found another spot that might have been an unmarked grave. The quiet that at first seemed peaceful now had a more sinister feel. She rubbed the goosebumps on the back of her neck. "It's chilly in here," she said. "Let's go."

"Good!" Zach said. He pushed through the underbrush back the way they had come. Odin reappeared, crashing through the bushes, tongue lolling. Burs clung to the fur along his back and hindquarters.

"Odin, where did you go?" Kaya asked, pulling at some of the burs.

"Your dog is smart," Zach said. "He didn't want anything to do with that place." As Zach scratched behind Odin's ears, Odin nosed his leg. Zach backed up a step, but Odin followed, focused on Zach's pocket.

"Odin!" Kaya said, shooing him away from Zach. "Sorry. He is usually not so rude."

"'s all right," Zach grinned. "There's something in there he wants. Come on, Nors- I mean, Kaya. Wanna catch some crawdads?"

A creek bed wound its way through the rear of the Spence property. Rough cracks in the low spots left telltale signs of where water had once been. Dead leaves and fallen limbs littered the ground. Kaya imagined this wasn't all that much of a creek, even during the wettest of springs. She was surprised when Zach led her to a little gully that actually contained some water. He dug in his pocket and brought out two long strings. Handing her one, he dug into his other pocket and retrieved some greasy white lumps. "Take some of this bacon fat and tie it onto your string."

It took her several tries but Kaya finally got the slippery bait tied securely onto the end of her string. Zach had already found a spot to sit and lowered his string into the water. "Try over here," he said. "This is usually a good spot for them."

Kaya sat on a fallen log at the creek's edge and dropped her string into the water below.

Zach shook his head and peered into the murk below. Suddenly his string jiggled. "Look at that," he whispered. "I think I got one." He waited for another tug on his line, then lifted it smoothly out of the water.

Kaya gasped at the bizarre creature on the end of Zach's string. It was about the size and shape of her pointer finger, with big eyes on either side of its head, legs and antennae flailing in the air. "What *is* that thing?" she said, leaning away from it as he dangled it in front of her.

"A crawdad. See those little claws? You gotta look out for those. Grab him right here," Zach pinched the creature along its back, behind his front legs. "Right here so they can't pinch you." He removed the crawdad from his line and held it out to Kaya for a closer look.

She peered at it from a safe distance. "What do you do with them?"

"Well, some people eat 'em. If we had time to go fishing, we could use 'em as bait. But today I think I'll just throw him back in." He gave the wriggling creature one last look before plopping him back into the silty creek water.

Almost immediately Kaya's line jerked. "You got one, too!" Zach said. "Wait until he's on good and tight. Good! Now lift him right out of the water, nice and easy."

She did as he said and another of the strange brownish creatures clung to her line as well. She held the string aloft with one hand and tried to remove it with the other. "Ouch!" she called out, yanking her hand back. "They *do* pinch!" she laughed. She tried again, using Zach's method of grasping the crawdad behind its front two legs. Pulling gently she removed it from the soggy bacon fat and inspected it closely. "It looks like a bug," she said. "Look at those feelers."

"Yep," Zach said. "Some people call them mud bugs."

"Mud bugs," Kaya repeated, turning the crawdad

this way and that. "I can just drop it back in the water?"

Zach nodded, so she held it over the water and let it go. It disappeared and she immediately dropped what was left of her bait back in the water.

The two of them spent a good while toying with their prey. Eventually Kaya looked up at the sun. "I better be getting back," she said.

"Oh. Sure," said Zach. "I'll show you a different way back to your place." He led the way and Kaya walked along beside him.

"I think we're coming to the camp meeting tonight, so maybe I will see you there. Does your father go to the camp meetings, too?"

Zach glanced sideways at her and looked away again. "My pa's been gone for a while. Don't know where."

"Gone? Does he have to travel for work? Sometimes Papa has to travel for his carpentry jobs."

"Sort of," Zach answered. "Pa's not like other folks. He doesn't raise cattle, or work in a store, or grow cotton. He just disappears, and comes back with money. He hunts and sells hides, rides for some of the big spreads - once he said he worked on a steamboat on the Red River. Went all the way to the ocean and back." Zach paused. "Sometimes he tells us where he's going. Sometimes, he doesn't. Ma doesn't say anything, but I can tell she's worried."

"How long has he been gone?"

Zach considered. "A few weeks, I reckon."

Kaya tried to remember if her father had ever been gone that long, and if her mother had been worried. She couldn't. "What are you going to do?"

Zach shrugged. "Nothing I *can* do. I just wish he would come home." They walked in silence. The trees thinned, and they gradually crossed into pastureland and full sun. The field smelled of parched grasses, hard-baked earth and cow patty. A light breeze rearranged the scattered leaves on the ground around them.

Zach passed a tuft of wild hay, dried out and long past the end of its growing season. He leaned down and broke off a single strand and put it between his teeth. The feathery tip bounced up and down as he chewed the opposite end. He noticed Kaya watching him. He broke off another and handed Kaya a piece. "Want one?" he offered.

She looked it over carefully, then took it and stuck it in her mouth. "It tastes like . . . nothing."

"You don't eat it," Zach explained. "Just something

to chew. Kaya? What happened to your ma?" When she didn't answer right away, Zach said, "You don't have to talk about it if you don't want to."

"I don't mind. She got shot."

"Shot! That's awful," Zach said. "I never heard of any woman getting shot."

"Her stage coach got robbed. Papa said it was just bad luck." Kaya glanced at Zach. "She said was on her way here because *Bestemor* was sick."

"Your grandma, sick? That's news to me."

Kaya nodded. "I don't think she was. But why else would Mama come here?"

"She grew up here, didn't she? Maybe she was visiting someone else."

"Maybe. But why not just say that?"

Zach shrugged. "My Pa never tells us what he's up to, either. I figure he doesn't think I need to know. Or doesn't want me to know."

Kaya stopped and stared off into the distance.

"What?" he said, stopping also, looking for whatever she was staring at.

"Nothing, it's just -" Kaya looked at Zach. "Thanks. That actually makes a lot of sense."

Zach's ears turned pink again. "Sure." He looked away first and they resumed walking. "Your ma just passed recently?" Zach said. "You don't seem too sad about it."

"I am sad," Kaya said. "But Papa doesn't like - I mean, we don't - we're not supposed to show it. But everything reminds me of her. So many things around the house, like her trunk or scraps of fabric in my quilt. Her horse, Dala." Kaya paused. "Sometimes it's almost like it was a dream, or it happened to someone else. Since we got here, there's so much to do, I go all day long and don't think of her until I go to bed. You want to know something strange?"

"Sure."

"She crossed thousands of miles of ocean when she came here from Norway, safe and sound. Then she died doing something people do all the time - visiting relatives."

Kaya and Zach struck out down the creek going opposite the way they had come. Their shadows lengthened in front of them as they made their way around fallen logs, stumps, rocks and rabbit holes. At last Zach turned away from the creek bed. "There's Belknap Road, on the other side of that pecan grove. It goes to Tyler," he said, pointing. "Our place is right through those trees."

Kaya heard him but her eyes locked onto something else. "Zach."

Zach kept walking.

"Zach." Louder, this time. "How long has it been since you came this way?"

"I dunno. Why?"

Kaya pointed across the creek bed. "Was that there?"

Zach's jaw dropped. "No sirree bob. It sure wasn't."

The two children approached, taking care where they stepped. "Maybe it's an animal," Kaya said.

Zach squatted next to the skeleton and picked up a tattered strip of fabric. "What kind of an animal wears clothes?" He dropped the cloth and wiped his hand on his pants. "Guess the scavengers have been here."

"Scavengers . . ." Kaya repeated. "Is that why there's only . . ." she pointed at their find.

"The ribs. Maybe if we spread out and look around, we'll find the rest of it."

Kaya nodded, her eyes locked on the bones. Zach stepped back and started searching the ground to his right.

"You take that side," he said. "Kaya?"

"Yes?"

"It's just bones. It won't hurt you."

"I know," Kaya said. "It's just that . . . I've never seen . . ." She knelt and touched the tip of one of the ribs on a spot that had been picked clean. It was smooth, like an antler. She pressed it, and, to her surprise, it gave a little. Kaya stood up quickly and vigorously rubbed her finger on her apron.

Zach was busy prowling the edge of the creek bed. Kaya began exploring the opposite side of the remains. She stepped over the clumping grass, careful not to crush anything that might lie hidden beneath. After a several minutes of inspecting the ground she stopped to stretch her aching neck. Kaya was about to call out to Zach, to remind him that she didn't know the way back to his place, when she stepped on something hard underfoot. Her heart started pounding as she imagined what might be there. A jaw bone? A finger? "Zach!"

She took a step back and spread the grass apart. Kaya reached out a trembling hand to pick up the thing, encrusted in dirt. She had to use her fingers to dig it free. She felt something hard, with edges. *This is no bone.* She brushed the dirt away.

"Kaya! Did you find something?"

She held out her hand to show him what she found. "Its broken. I think it's a pipe, but it's different from my Papa's."

"It's a corncob pipe," Zach said. "And look at this." He held the top half of a small glass bottle. The cork was still in it. A scrap of label clung to the front. "What does it say?" Zach peered at the label.

"I don't know," Kaya said. "It's too faded to read. Let's take it with us."

Zach dropped the glass into his pants pocket, then stood with his hands on his hips, surveying the scene. "One thing for sure – these bones aren't going anywhere." He laughed at his own little joke.

Kaya groaned.

Zach shrugged. "Sorry. We need to tell somebody about this. Let's go to my place. It's closer. We can come back tomorrow and investigate some more, if you want."

Kaya nodded. "All right."

"Wait 'til my ma hears what we found!" Zach said. He started off at a steady trot. Kaya stayed right behind him.

CHAPTER EIGHT

The Spence cabin sat back off a dirt road up against a scrubby stand of live oak trees. The decrepit barn leaned just right of center, chunks of shingles missing from the roof. Polka-dotted guineas pecked at the ground around the well near the front porch. To the left of the house the chopping block sat neglected. A rusty ax lay propped against one side of the stump, serving as a fine support for a large garden spider's web.

A woman sat in an old rocking chair on the far end of the porch, fanning herself with a tattered straw hat. She stopped rocking and sat forward when Kaya and Zach came tearing around the side of the Spence cabin.

"Ma!" Zach shouted.

"Zachary, what on earth? Your ma's not home. She walked over to the Olsons, looking for you, I suppose." The woman smiled at Kaya. "And who is this pretty thing?"

106

Zach stood with his hands on his hips and leaned forward at the waist to catch his breath. Kaya flopped onto the front steps. "Grandma, this is Kaya. Kaya, this is my Grandma Polly."

"Kaya Olson?" Polly Spence peered at her so intently, Kaya blushed and looked away.

"Grandma!"

Polly returned her attention to her grandson. "What is it, Zach?"

Zach looked to Kaya before continuing. When she nodded, the news burst out of him. "It's a body, Grandma!"

"What?"

"A dead body! Kaya found it out by the creek bed!"

"What kind of body?"

"It's a person, not an animal." Zach fidgeted with excitement, dancing back and forth like a dog imploring its master: *come on, follow me, it's important*!

"Are you sure it's not a deer? Or a cow?"

Both children nodded vigorously. "Yes, ma'am," Kaya said. "Zach found some bits of clothes on it." She remembered something else. "Zach, the bottle."

"Oh, yeah," Zach said. He reached into his pocket carefully and pulled it out by the top. He peered at the label again. "It's a Q, I think."

"Let me see that, Zach," Polly said. She inspected the scrap of paper and said, "It must be quinine. Can't think of anything else that would start with a Q."

"And there was a pipe!" Kaya dug the pipe remnants out of her apron pocket. She held it out for Polly to see.

Polly took the pipe and inspected it. "My stars," she said. She handed it back to Kaya.

"I'll go get Ma!" Zachary said, tearing out of the front yard and across the prairie.

"Zach!" Kaya called after him. "Wait!" She looked back at the elder Mrs. Spence, who shook her head and settled back into her chair.

"That boy. Wild as a March hare. I could point you in the right direction, but I would hate to send you out there by yourself, your being new here and all. Why don't you wait here? When Zach and his mother get back, we can see that you get home safe and sound."

Kaya hesitated. Now she had waited too long. She wanted to follow Zach, but she didn't want to appear rude to his grandmother. She would have to get used to Zach's habit of dashing off on his own.

"Why don't you come inside and wait. I need to give dinner a stir." Polly Spence reached for her cane and moved to the front door, holding it open. Kaya checked once more for any sign of Zach, but he had already disappeared. She forced a smile and followed Polly Spence inside.

The Spence cabin was a single room lit only by the glow of a small fire in the hearth. It was no bigger than Kaya's grandmother's side of their cabin. A kitchen table, some chairs and a cupboard were arranged on the left side near the fireplace. On the right side was a large bureau, and a bed big enough for two adults. The room was simple with split log walls and plank floors. A pole ladder led up to a loft overhanging half the lower room.

"Come in and have a seat," said Mrs. Spence, gesturing towards a three-legged stool near the hearth. "It's been so long since I had the company of a little girl," Polly continued. "It's been only boys around here, and rough customers at that."

Mrs. Spence was a grandmother also, but had little else in common with *Bestemor* Olena. Polly Spence was not much taller than Kaya and twice as round. Wisps of gray hair strayed from her bun. Scuffed shoes peeked from underneath the tattered hem of her short dress.

A black iron skillet sat on the hearth,warming its contents. There was the sweet smell of fresh cornbread, the tang of the peach cobbler with a golden crust cooling on the table, and the rich aroma of something left cooking all day emanating from the pot.

"Red beans," Mrs. Spence said as she stirred them. "Did you ever have red beans and cornbread?"

"Red beans? I - I'm not sure." *Mama never cooked beans. She said they were only fit for the livestock.*

"You never had *my* red beans. I cooked them all day with a ham hock. You're welcome to stay for supper. We have plenty. I always cook enough in case one of our wandering menfolk turns up."

The older woman's carved cane thumped as she navigated the small space, adjusting the small vase of Indian paintbrush flowers on the kitchen table, picking up a crumbling dead leaf from the floor and tossing it into the ashes. She clanked the lid back down on the pot and dragged a chair from the kitchen table closer to the hearth. Polly Spence sat down heavily and leaned her cane against the cabin wall. "It's all right, girl," she smiled again. "I won't bite. I don't have enough teeth left."

Kaya saw that there were indeed a few gaps in Mrs. Spence's smile.

"But you don't want to hear an old woman prattle on. Zach tells me you and your pa just moved back here from Normandy. I've never been to Normandy. Humor me and tell me about yourself, young 'un. Tell me about yourself and what Normandy is like."

So Kaya told Mrs. Spence all about Normandy, her mother and father, *Onkel* Otto and *Tante* Julia. She told her about her church, the Norwegian school, and the *Sittende Mai* celebrations.

"Oh yes," Mrs. Spence said. "That's like our Fourth of July."

"Well, yes," said Kaya.

"*Ja* is 'yes'. 'Hello' is easy – *hallo*. And 'thank you' is –

"*Mange takk*."

"Yes! *Mange takk*. You see? I still remember. There used to be many Norwegian families in Preston." Polly Spence turned her penetrating gaze on Kaya again. "You're such a pretty thing. The image of your mother, God rest her soul."

"My mother? You knew my mother?"

"Why, of course, dear. I knew your mother, and her parents, the Piersons, before they moved to Normandy."

"Because of the fever?"

"The fever?"

Kaya wondered if the older woman was hard of hearing, or dotty. "They moved to Normandy, because of the fever?" she repeated, a little louder. "That's what my teacher said, that lots of Norwegians moved away from Preston after the fever hit."

"Well, yes, your teacher's right about that. Some did. But not the Piersons. That was . . . that was later." Mrs. Spence busied herself with giving the beans another stir.

Kaya waited for her to continue, but Mrs. Spence didn't elaborate. Kaya remembered what Zach said, about her mother maybe visiting someone else in Preston. She also remembered what he said about adults and their secrets. Here was someone else who knew her mother, and no one else was around to shush her or change the subject. Kaya saw her chance, and she took it. "Mrs. Spence, did Mama - did she ever come and visit you here in Preston?

After she moved away?"

"All that way to visit an old woman? Heavens, no. What on earth gave you that idea?"

"Mama was on her way to Preston when she - when she died. She said she was coming to visit *Bestemor* because *Bestemor* was sick. But I asked *Bestemor*, and she hasn't been sick. So I thought maybe Mama was coming here to visit someone else, since she used to live here."

Polly Spence stopped stirring. "I haven't seen your mother since before you were born," she said softly, almost to herself. She tapped the spoon briskly against the inside of the pot and set it aside. Hands on her hips, she cocked her head to one side as she looked Kaya over once again. "You have your mother's hair, but I think you have your father's eyes. Just like young Zachary. Here," she said, brightening. "I have a picture of Zach's father, my son Jesse. See if you think I'm right."

Polly Spence reached for her cane and went to the bureau on the other side of the cabin. Opening a drawer, she felt around for a moment, then pulled something out. She made her way back to the hearth with a small black rectangle and handed it to Kaya.

Jesse Spence. Kaya's curiosity increased when she

remembered how agitated her father had been at the mention of his name. She opened the sturdy cardboard folder. Tucked inside was a picture of an unsmiling young man. He had a head full of curling hair that framed his square-jawed face. His bristling mustache hugged his upper lip. Dark eyes gazed defiantly at Kaya, the photographer, the world. "Yes, they do favor," Kaya said. "And I think they both have your eyes."

Polly Spence nodded. "Yes! Not everyone notices that, but I think so, too. That was taken when a picture fella came to town a few years ago. Jesse had some pictures made of himself and he gave one to me."

She took the picture back from Kaya. She stroked the cardboard frame affectionately. "He's no angel, but he loves his mother, my Jesse does. He made this cane for me." Mrs. Spence turned the cane this way and that, admiring it. "Jesse was always good with his hands. As long as he has something to do with his hands, he stays out of trouble. But sometimes he gets the urge to wander and he takes off. Just like his father. . ."

Mrs. Spence shifted in her chair and her son's picture slipped off her lap and onto the floor. "Oh dear," she said, and leaned down to retrieve it.

Kaya jumped up, eager to stretch her legs a little. "I'll get it, ma'am," she said.

"Thank you, dear," Mrs. Spence said, settling herself again. "It's so hard when you get to be my age, nothing but old bones and aches and pains."

Kaya picked up the picture and held it out to her.

"Would you be a dear and put it back for me?" Mrs. Spence pointed to the bureau on the other side of the room. "Just slip it into the drawer that I left open."

Kaya nodded and walked to the bureau. As she placed the picture back in the drawer, she gasped. A white dala horse lay in the drawer next to some lace collars. She reached down and picked it up. Except for the orange stripes where the blue should be, this was a twin of her mother's dala horse. She patted her apron pocket for her own dala horse, then remembered she had tucked it under her pillow for safekeeping before helping churn the buttermilk that morning.

"You found my little horse, I see," Mrs. Spence said. "Isn't it lovely? Jesse carved it for me." She smiled. "Everyone has a little good in them. Even someone as rowdy as Jesse."

Kaya stared at the horse. The guineas outside squawked, startling both of them.

"Sounds like they're back," Mrs. Spence said. "That was quick."

Kaya rushed to the front window. Soon three figures appeared in the distance. As they neared, she saw her father had accompanied Lucy and Zach.

Zach raced ahead of the adults and met Kaya inside the front door. "It's a human body all right," Zach said, his face flushed. "Your pa says so." He collapsed into a chair at the table.

Lars and Lucy followed on Zach's heels. Kaya heard their voices as they climbed the porch stairs. Lars held the door for Lucy. Lucy smiled at him as she passed through, and Lars held her gaze. Kaya tried to remember if she had ever seen him look at her mother that way.

Once inside, Lucy took in the scene. "Kaya, welcome! Zach said you were here. We were already on our way over when we ran into him. I hope you didn't have to wait too long."

Polly replied, "We were just getting to know each other. Kaya was telling me all about Normandy."

Lars removed his hat as he came inside.

116

"Afternoon, Miz Spence. Hello, Kaya. What's that you have there?" he said, squinting into the interior gloom to see what Kaya was holding. "Ah. A dala horse."

"What kind of horse?" Polly Spence asked. "Doll-ah?"

"Yes, dala horse," Lars repeated. "A toy. From the old country."

"I don't know about 'dala'. All I know is, Jesse made it for me years ago," Mrs. Spence said, reaching for the horse. Kaya handed it over. The old woman put it back in its drawer and pushed it closed.

"Well." Lars said. "I suppose we should be going."

"Won't you stay for supper?" Polly Spence asked. "I made a pot of beans."

"No, thank you," Lars said. "I just wanted to see these two home and collect Kaya. *Mor* will be wondering what became of us. I understand you are going to the camp meeting tonight?" Lars said to Lucy, who nodded. "We will see you there. Come along, Kaya."

Kaya gazed into the distance as they walked home. She gathered her courage to ask the question that had been troubling her ever since her conversation with Polly Spence. "Papa, did Mama know Zach's father?"

Lars did not answer right away. "Why do you ask?" he finally said.

"Mrs. Spence – the older one – her dala horse. Mama had one just like it."

Lars relaxed. "Kaya, those horses are everywhere in Norway. They all look alike. They're *supposed* to. Her son probably bought it from a Norwegian who needed to sell it for the money."

"But she said he made it."

"She's old, Kaya. Old people sometimes get confused."

"*Bestemor* is old, and she is never confused."

"That is certainly true. But Mrs. Spence is not *Bestemor*."

"But -"

"It's nothing, Kaya. Just another dala horse."

As they neared the Olson cabin, mouthwatering aromas greeted them.

"*Hallo*, you two," Olena said. "Did you get everything sorted out? Lars, you left in such a hurry, I didn't get any details."

"It's a long story," Lars said. "I will tell you everything, but first: what's for dinner?"

They sat together over a meal of fried chicken and sliced tomatoes. Kaya devoured two chicken legs, two slices of tomato and a glass of milk. Her father was a man who respected food too much to ever leave anything on his plate. Deep into his third helping, he finally showed signs of slowing down.

Kaya and her grandmother worked together cleaning up. "I think your father has a hollow leg," Olena said. "That must be where he puts all that food." She handed Kaya a wet dish.

Kaya giggled as she toweled it dry. "Mama always said – " she stopped in mid-sentence. *Mama.* She checked her stomach for flips and her heart for pounding, but they were both fine. She continued, "Mama always said the same thing."

Olena patted her shoulder with a damp hand, then continued with the dishes.

Lars looked up from his plate, fork in midair. "What?"

"Nothing, Papa," Kaya said. "Don't forget to save

room for dessert."

"There is always room for dessert," Lars replied seriously as he mashed the last crumbs from his plate with his fork and licked it clean.

Over a bowl of blackberry cobbler, Lars told his mother about the bones in the woods. At the end of his tale, Lars said, "They found a quinine bottle near the bones."

"And a pipe!" added Kaya. She dug it out of her apron pocket and handed it over.

"A corncob pipe." Olena sat back in her chair, eyebrows raised.

"What does it mean?" Kaya asked.

"Most Americans around here carry a twist if they are tobacco users. That fellow Granger that drove the freight wagon that got robbed - he smokes a corncob pipe."

"Sounds like Sheriff Bradley should know about this," Lars said.

CHAPTER NINE

That evening the Olsons attended their first-ever camp meeting. People came to the camp meeting from miles around. Wagons filled the broad prairie east of Preston. A tent stood staked above the prairie in the distance. Campfires flared, needed more for their light than their warmth. Kaya, Lars and Olena left their wagon well clear of the crowd and walked toward the tent. They passed many families enjoying the service while relaxing on blankets on the ground. Most had brought their supper along with them.

Lars found seats on a bench at the rear of the tent. "Is this all right for you, *Mor*?" he said, speaking over the exuberant singing. "I want to find the sheriff."

"Yes, thank you, Lars, and you are excused. I know this is not your favorite way to spend a free evening. We will meet you later back at the wagon."

"I'll see you there," Lars said, uneasy in the noisy

crowd. He made a hasty retreat.

"Don't worry," her grandmother said. "After he finds Sheriff Bradley, he is going over to smoke his pipe with the other men and talk about carpentry and weather and lots of other boring subjects."

Kaya smiled. "Yes, just like at home after church on Sundays." She settled into her seat and looked around. This was unlike any church service she had ever attended, and she had attended many. Normandy had a modest Lutheran church. They shared Pastor Swenson with Lutheran congregations in Brownsboro and Preston. Kaya attended services most Sunday mornings with her parents. *Tante* Julia and *Onkel* Otto were always there as well as most of the Norwegian families in town. The service was dignified and quiet, and Kaya knew more or less what to expect every week. Upon arrival, the women and children filed in and took their seats on the left side of the aisle. The men stood around outside chatting until Pastor Swenson arrived. When he did, they lined up on either side of the doorway, all nodding in greeting. Pastor Swenson led them inside. Once all were seated, he began the service in his Sunday best black cassock and white surplice, calmly leading the congregation through the many parts of the service such as the Kyrie, the Lord's Prayer, the Creed - all in Norwegian, of course. The congregants knew when to respond, when to kneel, when to rise and did so more or less in unison. During communion, those who had been confirmed meekly lined up to accept a bite-sized bit of flatbread on the tongue and a quick swallow of sacramental wine before quietly making their way around the outer aisles and back into their pews. The traditional Norwegian Lutheran service was reserved, restrained, refined. The camp meeting was quite the opposite.

The crowd sang lustily without benefit of choir or musical instrument. A scattering of 'Amen!' and 'Halleluja' fluttered through the tent as they ended their hymn. Then, a man at the front of the tent started preaching. He wore a light colored shirt and suit with a black string tie, no different from what any American man might wear, preacher or not. He paced back and forth, gesturing frequently with his bible. Sweat trickled from his hairline into his face, though he tried to keep dry with frequent swipes of his bright red handkerchief. Occasionally he shouted something at the crowd, and they responded with enthusiasm. Kaya could understand most of it, but with the interference from the crowd she had to guess at the rest. It was interesting enough watching the people around her. They seemed under the preacher's spell, hanging on his words and answering with more *Amens* and *Hallelujas*. Kaya and Olena exchanged a look. Olena shrugged her shoulders and they both returned their attention to the spectacle before them.

Now some of the men and women left their seats and lined up in the aisle to approach the preacher. A wave of murmurs surged through the crowd.

Kaya jumped when someone tapped her on the shoulder. "Hey, Norskie." Zach's gappy smile loomed behind her in the dark. "Just joshin'!" he said, hands raised in surrender, when he saw the look on her face.

"Hello, Zach," said Olena. "Where's your mother?"

"She's right there." Zach waved to his mother as she approached. Lucy Spence walked slowly toward them with Polly Spence on one arm. "Miz Olson, can Nor- I mean, can Kaya come play with us kids?"

"That sounds lovely, Zach." Olena turned to Kaya. "It would do you good to meet some more children your age." She patted Kaya's knee and got up to let her out of the cramped seating.

"Come on, Kaya," Zach said, heading back out the

rear of the tent. "Everybody's waiting."

Kaya glanced up at the front of the tent. The preacher had his hand on an older man's shoulder. He shouted something and waved his bible skyward. The older man keeled over, but the people around him caught him before he fell. A great cry went up from the crowd. She glanced back at Zach, who was still waving. Her stomach fluttered at the thought of going with him and meeting his friends, who were most likely all Americans. Kaya hesitated. She knew Zach was likely to bolt and leave her standing there if she didn't decide soon. She looked at her grandmother, and Olena nodded encouragingly. Kaya reached into her pocket. She had retrieved her dala horse from her room as soon as she returned from the Spence cabin that afternoon. Feeling the weight of it there now gave her courage.

Kaya squeezed by her grandmother and passed Lucy and Polly Spence on her way out of the tent. "Hello, Mrs. Spence," she said, dipping a quick curtsy.

"Hello – "

"Hello, Kaya." Both women had answered at once.

"Come on, Kaya!" Zach called, waiting outside the tent.

"Go ahead, dear," Polly Spence said, turning toward Zach and then back to Kaya. "We don't want to keep you from your play."

"Better go, Kaya," Lucy agreed. "Zach is liable to leave you behind."

"Don't I know it," she said under her breath. "Thank you," she said a little louder to the two Mrs. Spences and gave another abbreviated curtsy as she left. At last she caught up with Zach.

"This is a funny town," she said to him as they walked through the adults passing them on their way towards the tent.

"Funny how?"

"Everyone seems to know me, or know about me, and I have never been here before in my life. Everyone knows my grandmother. And your mother knows my father. And earlier today, your grandmother said she knew my mother."

"What's so funny about that? They all used to live here."

"Mama never talked about her life in Preston, like it never happened. It's strange finding out about a whole other life she had before me."

126

"Grown-ups are funny that way. You never know what stuff they'll decide needs to be kept secret." Zach's eyes darted to Kaya as they walked along in silence. "You should thank me," he said, changing the subject.

"Why?"

"It was about to get wild in the tent. They were lined up for the healing. They'll be at it all night."

"Healing?"

"Sure. The preacher asks anyone who needs healing to come up front and he lays his hands on them and makes them better."

"Just with his hands?"

"Yep. They fall down and have fits and everything. He really puts on a show."

"Have you seen him before?

"Maybe not him, but other jackleg preachers just like him."

Zach headed for a spot where the prairie blended into a more wooded area. "There they are," he said. "Hey, Sam. Hey, everybody."

Dim forms in the twilight approached and resolved into several children. They came toward her to get a closer look. Kaya stood stiffly, preparing her for another round of strangers calling her 'Norskie', and having to prove to all of these Americans that just because she spoke Norwegian didn't mean she couldn't speak English.

"This here's the new girl I was telling you about," Zach said. "Her name's Kaya."

Kaya's head swiveled to Zach. He grinned at her and continued with his introductions. "This is Tom. This is Georgie, and over there is Emily. The tall one is Josephine, but everybody calls her Jo."

The kids nodded toward her and murmured greetings. The girls approached first. Jo said, "Hi, Kaya. We were about to play hide and seek. You can stay with Emily and me since you don't know your way around yet." Jo took Kaya's hand, Emily took the other. Jo turned to Zach and said, "Boys against the girls! You're it!" Jo and Emily raced into the woods, pulling Kaya along with them.

"Dang it, Jo!" Zach shouted after them. "It was our turn to hide!" The boys began counting to twenty and the game was on. Kaya stayed close to Jo and Emily for fear of becoming lost. Eventually she recognized the same strangely shaped tree here or a dry creek bed there and began enjoying herself as they ran back and forth in the dark. Three long rounds of hide-and-seek later, the five agreed to take a break. They collapsed on the ground together, giggling and trading insults. Suddenly a branch snapped loudly. They peered into the dark woods around them, startled.

"Well, well, what do we have here?" a voice sneered.

CHAPTER TEN

A tall form emerged from the woods and stood over the group. "Frank!" said Zach. "Criminy! You scared us."

"That's not hard to do to a bunch of runts like you," said Frank. He wore his broad-brimmed hat cocked back on his head. His thumbs were tucked into a holster complete with revolver. Spurs clinked on his boots, and he wore a large kerchief around his neck. He swaggered among the children, inspecting them as if they were prize calves at the county fair. "I do declare. It's the Clark kid," he said, kicking Tom's shoe. "Hey kid – did your daddy ever pay my old man the money he owed him?"

Tom gaped at Frank. Before he could answer, Frank said, "I didn't think so. And looky here – it's George Wells. Is that pretty sister of yours still at home, Wells?"

"None of your business," Georgie muttered.

"What? What did you say?" Frank reached down and twisted Georgie's shirt tightly at the collar.

"Sure, sure, Frank," Georgie choked. "She's still at home."

"That's what I thought you said." Frank released Georgie and kept walking until he got to Kaya. He bent down to peer into her face. "Who might you be, little missy?"

Kaya was too stunned to speak. Zach came to her rescue. "Lay off, Frank. She's new in town. She's Miz Olson's granddaughter."

Frank's head swiveled toward Zach. "Olson!" he said. He turned back to Kaya. "Olson," he repeated. "Not Lars Olson? He your pa? Alma your ma?"

Kaya could only stare at this rude person. Zach and the other children knew him. But who was he?

"I guess that means you're Norskie. Can't speak English?" he sneered.

"Sure she can, Frank. Good as you or me."

"Shut up, Zach. Let her do her own talking. Well, can you speak English or not?"

Kaya nodded. "Yes, I speak English."

Frank reached toward Kaya. She stepped back, out of his reach. He matched her step. In a flash, his hand shot out. Rough fingers cupped Kaya's chin, tilted her face up and peered at her intently. Kaya yanked her head back and glared at him. "Huh," Frank said to himself. He walked a tight circle around her as if he were looking for something.

"How old are you?"

"What?"

"You said you speak English," he snarled. "*How old?*"

"T-ten."

"T-ten?" Frank mocked. He cocked his head at her. "Well I'll be damned," he said softly. A crafty look came over his face. "Looks like you kids have been having some fun tonight. Want to have some more fun?" He eyed the group around him. "Well, do ya?"

No one said a word. He snickered at their silence. "Thought you might like that. Everybody up. What we need us is a good old-fashioned snipe hunt. You know what that is, right?"

The others nodded half-heartedly.

"Good. Now listen here, New Girl. Since you are new in our town, we want to make you the guest of honor in our snipe hunt."

"No, Frank!" Zach cried. "Leave her alone!"

"Whatsa matter, Zach?" Frank teased. "Sweet on

her already?"

Zach ran toward Frank, fists raised. Frank pushed him down, hard. He clicked his tongue disapprovingly. "Zach, you should know better than that. Now – where's our New Girl? Do *you* know what to do, New Girl?"

Kaya shook her head 'no'.

"Didn't think so. Snipe is a local critter, real good eatin' but can be a little frisky. Big teeth. The best way to catch one is for us to beat these here bushes and flush one out. We're gonna to let you be the snipe catcher. When we flush him out and you hear him runnin' toward you, smash him over the head with your snipe stick. You do have your snipe stick, don't you?"

Kaya had no idea what a snipe was, but from Zach's reaction, she didn't think she wanted anything to do with one. "I won't," she said.

"You won't?" Frank snorted. "Did I hear you right?"

"I won't," Kaya repeated, louder.

Frank laughed shortly. "She says she won't." He shook his head. "Listen here, kid. You're new here, so maybe you don't know, but when I say you'll do something, you do it or else. Now, let's go." He made a grab for Kaya's arm. She jerked away from him and kicked him on the shin as hard as she could.

"Hey!" Frank yelped. He reached down to rub his leg. In mid-motion, his arm snaked around Kaya's waist. He clamped a hand over her mouth before she could make a fuss. Zach got up and ran at Frank again. Frank swung an elbow and connected with Zach's forehead, knocking him to the ground.

"Like I said, boy - you should know better." Shifting Kaya to one hip, he started farther into the woods. "Everyone spread out," he called over his shoulder. "I'll pick out a good spot for our snipe catcher here. Make some noise, drive the critter toward her, and we'll have us a snipe before you know it."

"No, Frank! Bring her back! Frank!" Zach called after them. "Frank!"

Frank ignored Zach's pleas. He trotted off, carrying Kaya for what seemed like an eternity. Her head pounded from the blood that had rushed there due to her awkward position. She struggled to breathe through her nose with Frank's hand clamped over her mouth. Something hard ground into her, trapped between her side and Frank's bony hip. Her father's words about how to survive being taken by Indians came back to her: *"If you fight back and are too much trouble, they will kill you on the spot."*

When she thought she could stand it no longer, Frank stopped and dropped Kaya face-down on the hard ground. His hands prodded her. "What *was* that thing?" he said as he reached into one of her pockets. "It was digging into me all the way out here." He withdrew the white dala horse from her pocket and inspected it carefully. "Aren't you a little old for toys?"

Kaya ignored him as she rolled over to sit up.

"Want it back?"

Kaya nodded, almost in tears.

"Too bad." He stuck the horse in the pocket of his leather vest. "Stand up," he said, grabbing Kaya's arm. "Hold still and you won't get hurt." He began untying the kerchief around his neck. Her father's advice deserted her as she saw an opportunity to escape. Quick as lightning, Kaya twisted away from Frank and tore off into the dark. Frank cursed loudly and dashed after her. After three quick strides, he dove for her and his momentum slammed them both to the ground. Frank landed on top of Kaya with a *whoof*, knocking the breath out of her. As Kaya lay gasping for breath, Frank straightened and sank a knee into her back.

"Hurts, don't it?" he panted. "Now I'll tell you again – *hold still.*" He wrapped the kerchief over her eyes and tied it behind her head.

"Wha – what – "

"Shut it, girlie. I've had enough of you. This little fandago is starting to be more trouble than it's worth." He stood her up and led her by the arm. They stopped. She smelled horse, heard it nicker. Kaya struggled against Frank's grip, causing him to grip her even harder. Jerking her hands together in front of her, he tied them together with some rope from his saddle. "No more sass from you tonight, or it will be the last time. Understand me?" He yanked on the rope, ripping her wrists raw.

Tears filled here eyes. Kaya blinked them away into the handkerchief and nodded silently. Maybe her father's advice was best, after all.

"Speak up, girl."

"Yes!" Kaya spat.

Frank laughed. "You've got spirit, I have to hand it to you. Now you and I are going for a ride. Are we going my way, or the hard way?"

Kaya squeaked out, "Your way."

"Smart girl. I'm going to lift you up, and you do the rest." His hands circled her waist and he half threw her onto the horse. He shoved her right leg across the saddle. "For crying out loud, you act like you never rode a horse before." The saddle leaned and creaked as Frank climbed up behind her. "Behave yourself on Dagger here. I'd hate for him to get spooked and buck you off."

Kaya's stomach clinched. Frank had read her mind. He reached around her for the reins, clicked to Dagger and said, "Don't worry, Norskie. It's not far."

They set off at a trot. Kaya clung to the saddle horn with her bound hands as she bounced along, terrified. The blindfold, the horse ride – *where could they be going?* Her mind raced, deciding which was the best way to survive this ordeal. She settled on sticking with her father's advice for now.

Dagger carried the extra weight easily. Frank spoke no further and Kaya certainly had nothing to say. With her eyes covered, her ears strained to make up for her lack of sight. They moved along briskly to sounds of horse hooves on packed earth, breaking twigs, the creaks of the saddle. Soon Frank spurred Dagger into a gallop and they pounded along quickly for a few minutes. Then Frank pulled on the

reins slightly and said, "Whoa, fella, whoa." Dagger
slowed to a walk and Frank called out, "It's me, boys."

Another voice answered from up ahead. "Who's
'me'?"

"Frank, you idiot."

Kaya turned toward the sounds of others - footsteps
on the hard ground, dishware clinking, the smell and
crackle of a campfire. Frank reined in Dagger and
dismounted. Once again he reached around her waist and
lifted her as easily as if she were thistledown.

"What's this?" the other voice said. "You brought us
a kid? I thought you went into town for some buck and
ball."

"Shut up, Cy," Frank said. "I got your shells."
Something clattered to the ground. "The girl ain't none of
your business. This is between me and my pa." Frank took
Kaya by the elbow and steered her forward. She stumbled
along with him until he stopped her. The heat of a campfire
drifted over from her left. Frank fumbled the kerchief off
her head. The knot had become tangled in her hair and she
yelped when he yanked it free. "The blindfold comes off
but not the rope," Frank said. "I know your tricks. We
won't be here long and I don't want to have to chase you

down and re-tie you."

Kaya rubbed her eyes with her still-tied hands. She stood in one corner of a cavernous barn. Stalls lined both sides, fading away into the dark interior. On their end a small fire crackled nearby, the earth around it cleared of hay and anything else that might catch fire too easily. Saddlebags and a tripod of rifles sat off to one side. To her right, a dozen crates marked '*QUININE*' sat stacked against the wall of the stall. Smaller light-colored canvas drawstring bags full to bursting lay piled next to the crates. There was writing on the bags, but it was too faint in the firelight for Kaya to read.

Beside the bags a man sat on the ground, propped against a saddle. His chest was wrapped with a bandage. A large dark stain spread across its middle. The man appeared to be asleep.

"Pa?" Frank said gently. He knelt near the injured man. "Pa, it's Frank. I brought you somethin'."

The man raised his head slowly and opened his eyes. "Frank," he said softly. "You brought me . . ."

"Don't wear yourself out, Pa. Let me talk." He stood and grabbed Kaya's arm, pulling her closer. "Do you know who this is?"

The man glanced up at Kaya dimly. He frowned. "You brought . . . a kid . . . here?" He winced and reached for his bandage. Frank stopped him. "Pa, this is – " he turned back to Kaya. "What's your name again?"

"Kaya," she answered. She had moved beyond her fear into an unnatural sense of calm. Being kidnapped, then tied up, blindfolded, thrown atop a horse, and brought to this place by a rough American – this was all a bad dream. *What did they want with her?*

"This is Kaya Olson, Pa. Alma's daughter."

Kaya whipped her head around to stare at Frank after he spoke her mother's name. But Frank's gaze was fixed on his father. Kaya turned back to look at the man. His eyes were fully open now, completely focused on Kaya. Dark eyes burned into hers, his wavy hair three haircuts too long spiking wildly around his face. Something tugged at Kaya's memory. As she struggled to reclaim it, the man spoke.

"Alma . . ."

"Alma's girl, Pa," Frank confirmed.

"Alma's girl." The man reached toward her. "Closer," he whispered. Frank yanked her arm again and she dropped to her knees next to the older man. He reached out a grimy hand and she backed away. Frank blocked her from moving back any further. The injured man touched her face lightly with his rough fingertips.

"Look here, Pa," Frank said. He dug the dala horse out of his pocket and handed it over. The man turned it over and over, straining to see in the dim light. Then he looked at Kaya with renewed interest.

"Yes, I see her . . . in you," he gasped slowly. He sat staring for a long moment. "She said . . . you favored."

"She said?" Kaya whispered, unbelieving. An injured man, hiding in a barn, who appeared to be part of a group of men up to no good, was the third stranger in the space of a few hours who claimed to know her mother. Kaya's head spun. *Impossible!* "You knew my mother?"

Frank chortled behind her. The injured man gave him a hard look. "Shut up, Frank," he wheezed. His eyes returned to Kaya. He blinked slowly. "Knew her," he said softly. His eyelids drooped. "Knew . . . " he smiled, and his head slowly sagged down and his chin rested on his chest. Frank felt his father's forehead, then leaned him back gently onto the saddle.

"He's hurt bad," Frank said softly. His angry features softened.

"What's wrong with him?" Kaya asked quietly.

Frank opened his mouth to answer, then clamped it shut. Instead he said, "Come on. We better get you back before somebody sets the sheriff on us."

Kaya stood up and turned to leave. "Wait," Frank said. He slipped the blindfold back over her eyes and led her back out of the barn the way they had come. "One of you go check on him," Frank said. "He's out again."

"Sure, Frank," a man answered. Boots crunched along the hay as the man did as he was told.

Kaya stiffened as they stopped. But this time, when Frank lifted her, she knew enough to swing her leg over and get seated in the saddle. Frank soon followed. Kaya barely had time to grab the saddle horn before Frank wheeled them around and they sped off, much faster than they had come.

Kaya's thoughts swirled. She kept coming back to the same question: why did this Frank person take her to see his father? The man was seriously hurt and needed a doctor. Why was he hidden away in an old barn instead of at home in bed? And why did he think he knew her, and her mother? Maybe he was so sick he was talking crazy. But that didn't explain why Frank also knew the names of both her parents.

As Kaya sorted out all of this new information, Frank suddenly reined up Dagger and jumped down. He set Kaya on the ground and untied her. She pushed the blindfold up and he snatched it off her head. He leaned down until their noses were almost touching and looked at her with his father's penetrating gaze.

"You a smart girl?" he asked.

Kaya nodded.

"Good." Frank reached for a small scabbard at his hip and drew out a knife. He thumbed the sharp edge. "Sure would be a pity if a smart girl got stupid and started flappin' her gums about a hurt man she met one night. You never know when you, or your pa, or your grandma, might have an accident. Like getting themselves shot in broad daylight." He held her eyes until he was satisfied she got his meaning. "All right, then. This never happened." He leaped onto Dagger and with a sharp "Yah!" he disappeared into the night.

Too late, Kaya found her voice. "Wait! Why did you take me?" she yelled after him. "Why me?"

Kaya stood perfectly still, listening to Frank's

retreat. When she was sure he was gone, her knees went weak with relief. She sat clumsily on the hard ground and looked around to see if she recognized anything from the earlier hide-and-seek game. Ashy clouds stretched across the sky, blocking any light from moon or stars. Kaya remembered her father's advice during their move to Preston: *just try not to get caught in unfamiliar territory on a cloudy night.* Now she knew why.

She heard faint sounds - *the camp meeting?* - but could not tell which direction they were coming from. Something rustled behind her. "Who's there?" she called. Only silence answered. At every chirp, every snap, every breath of wind she jumped and started, jerking her head wildly from side to side, seeing little even now that her eyes had adjusted to the velvet dark.

Think, Kaya! You can't just sit here. Have to get back to the meeting. Have to get back to the wagon. She picked a direction and started walking carefully, both hands held out in front of her. Twigs grabbed at her hair. Vines reached for her skirt. Tripping over sticks and stones, she shuffled her feet along the ground to keep from falling. Every bush was a wild snipe ready to attack, fangs bared and claws flashing. Every tree was Frank, reaching for her with his ropy arms. The hair rose on her neck until it felt it would detach itself completely and go floating off into the night. Rubbing it repeatedly did no good.

Kaya's nerves stretched to the breaking point. She thought of Ole Foss. "Faster, Kaya," she said to herself, now adding Indians to the list of things she was desperate to avoid. Ignoring branches and brambles, ignoring sure footing, she found herself interested in a trot rather than a walk. Soon her fear demanded she move faster, and she found herself running through the woods in a panic. An owl hooted, its wings disturbing the air above. Something brushed her hair and she cried out. Her foot caught a tree root and she went flying. "*Snipe!*" she thought, before her head hit the ground and she thought no more.

CHAPTER ELEVEN

Kaya dashed through unfamiliar woods. The sun directly overhead told her she was late for school. She knew she should hurry, but she did not know the way. She tried to run in a straight line as she had been taught by her father, but she kept passing the same tree. Lightning had struck it at some time in the past. One side was exactly right; the other had been neatly sheared away as if hewn by a giant's axe and lay decaying on the ground. Kaya paused to catch her breath, hands on her hips, chest heaving. She searched for some hint of the right direction and noticed the trees around her were not trees at all. They had changed into enormous carved wooden horses. White, orange, blue, red, yellow - their bright colors delighted Kaya as she looked up to take them all in. PLOP! A fat raindrop hit her on the forehead. Then another, and another as a summer shower began. Kaya sprang from

horse to horse seeking shelter under their smooth bellies,
but it didn't seem to matter. The moisture found her
wherever she went. She reached up to wipe her face with
her sleeve . . .

And opened her eyes. A familiar furry muzzle
continued licking her face.

"Hello, Odin. That's enough licking." Kaya tried to
push herself up. "Ow!" she exclaimed, testing the
throbbing spot on the right side of her forehead. The lump
was smaller than the goose egg people always used to
describe these injuries, but it was big enough to hurt. Kaya
suddenly remembered where she was and how she got
there. She hugged her dog. "Boy, am I glad to see you."

Odin tolerated the hug. With one last lick, he
wrestled free and made a few quick, urgent barks. Voices
filtered through the woods.

"Odin! Where are you, boy?"

"Kaya!"

"Kaya Olson!"

Lights flickered in the distance as searchers waved
their torches.

"Here! Here I am!" Kaya tried to stand. Her legs
wobbled. She sagged back against the tree that had tripped

her up earlier.

Odin stood next to her and barked once more. A large shadow solidified into her father as he rushed to her.

"Kaya! *Takk Gud*! We have been searching everywhere for you."

Kaya took a step forward on wobbly legs.

Her father snuffed out his torch and set it aside. He scooped up Kaya in his arms. "Here she is," he called out. "Odin found her." He turned to Odin and said, "*God hund, Odin. God hund*." Odin wagged his tail and yipped twice in acknowledgment. "Are you all right, Kaya?"

"My head hurts," she said. "I think I bumped it when I fell."

"Don't worry," said Lars. "We'll have you home safe and sound before you know it." He hugged her close. Kaya snuggled into his strong arms, breathing in his clean, familiar scent of lye soap and sweet pipe tobacco.

Olena Olson arrived next. She patted Kaya and fussed over her. Zach rushed in, his mother close behind. "Boy, am I glad to see you!" he said. This close, even in the dark Kaya could see the side of his face starting to swell where Frank had elbowed him. He touched her hand hesitantly and whispered, "Are you okay? Did Frank-"

Before Zach could finish, Lucy Spence said, "For heaven's sake, Zachary Spence, give the girl some room to breathe." She gently pulled him a step back, breaking their contact. "Kaya, are you all right? You gave us quite a scare."

You think YOU were scared. "I bumped my head, but I think I'm okay," she said, looking at Zach as she answered his mother. Zach's shoulders relaxed as he exhaled.

"Can you walk to the wagon, Kaya? We're quite a ways out."

"Yes, Papa, I think so."

On the way back, Olena walked alongside Lars and Kaya, patting her hand and murmuring comforts. Lucy and Zach walked ahead, Zach stealing guilty glances back at Kaya. From the adults' conversations Kaya learned the elder Mrs. Spence had gotten a ride home with another family.

At last they arrived at the camp meeting clearing. The meeting had ended for the night. Only two wagons remained, the Olsons' and the Spences'.

"Can you sit up, Kaya? I don't want you bouncing around back there in the empty wagon."

"I think so, Papa," Kaya replied weakly.

"Good girl. You can sit between us for the ride home." Lars lifted her into the wagon seat. Then he helped Olena up. She took her seat and put her arm around the exhausted girl.

"Thank you for helping us look for her," Lars said to the Spences as he climbed into the wagon.

"Will she be all right, Lars?" Lucy Spence asked. Zach stood next to her, looking at his feet.

"I don't know. We'll take her home where we will have better light to see that bump on her head."

"Oh, dear. Please let me know if I can do anything for you." Lucy peered up at the wagon. Lars tipped his hat in answer, and the Spences headed for their own nearby wagon.

"Up here, boy." Lars swatted the bed of the wagon behind him and Odin leapt up. "You get the back all to yourself tonight." Lars rubbed Odin's head affectionately. The dog's tail wagged madly and he barked his happy bark again. "That's right, boy. I'll find you a nice juicy bone when we get back." Lars flicked the reins and they headed home.

Kaya's feather bed was heaven. Her father and grandmother fussed around her with hot beef broth, fresh milk, and cool compresses for her head. "Is that better, dear?" Olena asked as she touched the compress to Kaya's bump.

"Yes, thank you."

Lars knelt beside his daughter. "Kaya, you must be more careful. You don't know your way around here yet, especially in the dark. We were so worried about you when Zach came and told us you were lost. What happened?"

Kaya recalled Frank's piercing eyes, his father lying wounded in the barn, the sharp edge of Frank's knife. She glanced away. "I . . . I don't remember."

Lars and Olena exchanged a concerned look. "Try to think, dear," Olena said. "Zach said Frank showed up out of nowhere and took you on a snipe hunt."

Lars grumped at the mention of Frank.

"Zach came after you," Olena continued, "but he couldn't find you in the dark, so he came and got us. We looked for you, too. Your father came back here to fetch Odin. Once Odin caught your scent, he found you right away."

So. They already know about Frank. Kaya knew she had to choose her words carefully. She had no doubt if she said anything about what happened, Frank would find out about it. She swallowed hard. She couldn't remember ever telling a blatant, deliberate lie. She wasn't sure she could do it right. "Yes, the snipe hunt. I – I tried to find my way in the dark but I fell down and bumped my head. That's - that's all I remember until Odin found me." She stammered out her story and waited for them to pick it apart. But the adults seemed not to notice her nervousness.

"A boy his age, taking a young girl on a snipe hunt? Ridiculous!" Lars stood up quickly. He paced the room like a hungry panther. "*Mor*, how old is Frank Spence now – seventeen?"

"More like twenty," said Olena.

"Frank *Spence*?" said Kaya. "Is Frank related to Zach?"

"Yes, dear," said Olena. "They are half-brothers. Frank's mother died when he was a baby. Zach's grandmother Polly raised him after that."

"I guess the apple doesn't fall too far from the tree," Lars growled.

Olena shook her head from side to side slowly.

152

"No, it doesn't. That boy is such a burden on his grandmother."

Frank was Zach's brother? That meant the man Kaya met tonight was Zach's father, too. Suddenly she pieced together what had eluded her earlier. The dark eyes, the unruly hair staring out from Polly Spence's picture – it was definitely the wounded man. But what was he doing hiding in that barn, with the bandaged wounds and strange men keeping watch over him? And how did he know her mother?

Lars stomped across the room and retrieved his hat from a peg on the wall.

"Where do you think you're going?" Olena asked.

"I'm going to have a word with that young whelp. We'll see if he ever lays a finger on Kaya again."

Kaya sat up quickly. "Papa, no!" Both adults turned to her, surprised at her outburst. "It's too dark," she added. "You might get lost, too."

Lars snorted.

"She's right, Lars." Olena warned. "You musn't go. And not because you might get lost. Frank is as unpredictable as his father. You've been in Normandy for so long, surrounded by other Norwegians. It's different here. Some Americans still resent us, especially after the war."

"But *Mor* – it's not right, what he did."

Olena Olson walked over to her son. "No, it isn't. But Kaya is here with us now, safe and sound. After what happened to your own father, Lars . . . you of all people should know we have to be careful."

"I suppose you're right, *Mor*. Anyway, no sense looking for him in the middle of the night. He's probably halfway to the Red River by now." He replaced his hat on its peg and returned to the chair at Kaya's bedside. Olena nodded, satisfied, and left the room.

"Is that why Frank . . . is that why he took me, Papa? Because I'm Norwegian?"

Lars shrugged and gestured with open hands. "Who knows, Kaya? I suppose it is possible. But I think it is more likely that Frank is a bully, and he was picking on you tonight because you are new in town."

Olena soon returned with a platter of cookies."Enough of this talk about Frank Spence. These should lift your spirits. This was my mother-in-law's recipe," she said, offering one to Kaya. After Kaya took one, she set it on a small table near the bed. "When we moved to America, Andreas – your *Bestefar* - insisted that I learn to make them just like hers." She smiled sadly. "He did love his *sandbakkels*. That was one thing from home he didn't want to miss."

Kaya bit into the crumbly sweet. "Is there anything from Norway that you miss, *Bestemor*?" she asked, eager to steer the conversation away from any more questions about her experience with Frank Spence.

"A good question, Kaya! I have such plenty here – beef, lamb, poultry, fresh fruits and vegetables. But I must admit, I miss a good piece of salmon. Fresh out of the sea and smoked over a good fire. Delicious!"

"What's salmon?"

"It's a big fish," Olena said, gesturing with her hands to show how big.

Kaya's eyes widened. "That's as long as Odin!"

"Sometimes bigger! But there are none here," Olena continued. "They live in the ocean. There are plenty of other kinds of fish here, but a salmon . . . " she stared into space for a moment, remembering. " A salmon is the finest fish, I think. Its flesh is a pink color, with a hint of orange. It is delicious smoked, with some nice potatoes or maybe some rice pudding. It makes me think of home."

"What do *you* miss about Norway, Papa?" Kaya said.

"I was just a boy when we came here," Lars said. "I hardly remember the trip, much less anything before that."

"*Bestemor*, tell me about Norway," Kaya said.

Lars groaned. "Now you've done it, Kaya. We will be up all night with these tales." He took a *sandbakkel* from the plate on the table.

"Shame on you, son. The girl wants to hear about our homeland. It is our duty to instruct her." Olena's eyes twinkled. "I supposed you've heard about the mountains and the snow?"

Kaya nodded.

"Did your father tell you about the fjords?"

"Not Papa, but - fee-*yords*? Where the water meets the land?"

"Yes, something like that. What about the lakes, crystal clear and deep as the sea?"

Kaya shook her head 'no'.

"The midnight sun? The whales? The corrupt upper classes?"

"*Mor* . . ." Lars said over a mouthful of cookie.

"Well Lars, what on earth *did* you tell her about?

Never mind. I know my granddaughter will appreciate my stories. Won't you, dear?"

Kaya nodded eagerly until her bump started to ache, stopping her mid-nod.

Lars shook his head, licking a few crumbs from his fingers. "You go ahead, *Mor*." He scooted his chair back, reached for a nearby footstool, and leaned back with his hands folded over his stomach, and closed his eyes.

Olena sat on the bed next to Kaya. Kaya relaxed into the pillows behind her head. "Norway is as different from Texas as can be." Olena began. "It is a beautiful place, Kaya. Cold, but beautiful. Texas can be beautiful, too, but in a different way.

"I grew up in a cozy cottage not much bigger than this room, a few minutes' walk from the sea. My father was a minister. His parish was in the south of Norway. Did you know, Kaya, that when you live near the sea, you can always feel it and smell it in the air? A hint of moisture, like it is here before a thunderstorm."

Kaya shook her head and waited for her grandmother to continue.

"There are many mountains in Norway, as you know. They are so tall, wherever you go, you can see them, whether they are near to you or far way. So high you think they might touch the sky. . . they can be the deepest blue, or a dark velvety green, or rosy at dawn, or purple at dusk – always changing colors in the light and shadows. Most of them are tipped with white from the snow on their peaks, so cold up there that it never completely melts away. When the mountains are near the sea, they are intertwined with ocean inlets – the fjords your father forgot to mention. It is as if the mountains are plunging their fingers into the sea."

"It sounds wonderful, *Bestemor*. But –" Kaya hesitated.

"Yes, dear?"

"If it was so beautiful, why did you leave?"

Olena glanced at Lars, who was now pretending to be asleep. "Well, now, that is a good question." She took a moment to organize her thoughts. "Norway is a good-sized country, Kaya, but it cannot compare with the size of America. There were too many people there, and not enough land to go around." Olena noted Kaya's puzzlement. "Ah, you have always lived in Texas, where there is nothing but land stretching as far as the eye can see. In Norway, this is not so. Let me show you." She reached for a coffee cup and saucer on the bedside table. "Imagine this cup and saucer is Norway. The cup is the mountains, and see this bit of saucer sticking out around the cup?"

Kaya nodded.

"That's the only land flat enough to farm. So you see, even though Norway is a large country, there is little land available for people to make a living." She lifted the cup and removed the saucer. She then set the cup back on the table. "In America, there are mountains." She tapped the cup. "But here there is so much more usable land," she spread her hands over the rest of the table top, "I don't think I can imagine it ever filling up."

"Is that why you came here? Because you were running out of land in Norway?"

"Yes, that was the main reason. Your *Bestefar* Andreas and I had a friend who had traveled to America. He kept in touch with us over the years, writing letters about everything he saw here. He wrote to us about plentiful land, fertile and cheap. Why, our parcel here is ten times, even twenty times larger and than anything any of us had in Norway. And all we had to do to get it was claim the land and pay the survey fees.

159

"Our friend urged us to come and, finally, we agreed. We sold our small farm in Norway and most of our belongings. Andreas booked passage for the four of us. Your *Onkel* Otto and *Tante* Julia came, too, and Mr. Bakken and his family. We thought it was a fine opportunity."

"And Mama was on the ship with you, wasn't she?"

Olena smiled sadly and nodded. "Yes, your mama was a little thing, about five, I guess. Just as pretty as you are now. She came with her parents of course - the Piersons - and her baby brother Olaf. We all came together. We set sail in April of 1847 and by July we had arrived in New Orleans."

"July? Why, that's-" Kaya counted on her fingers. "- three months! Three months on a ship?"

"Yes, three months. Norway is far from here, Kaya. It is across a vast ocean."

"What did you do all that time?"

"Mostly we were just anxious to arrive here. Once we were out to sea, one day was much like another. Our ship sailed from Norway to France to New Orleans. The weather was good, for the most part. We watched the sea and the clouds. The men tried to fish from the side of the ship, but it was difficult being so high off the water. I brought some books to read. The children ran races around the deck when they could stay out of the way of the crew, or wrestled with each other, or climbed all over everything, as young children like to do." Olena smiled as Kaya nodded in agreement. "Those who brought along their fiddles and their flutes would often favor us with a song or two. We would dance, or the men would serenade us. We even celebrated *Syttende Mai* on board, with *lefse* and salted herring and boiled potatoes. "

"Where did you sleep, *Bestemor*?" Kaya asked.

"We all had our own areas below decks. There was no room for beds, but we had plenty of clean straw to spread out and sleep on. We were right there along with the goats and the sheep and the chickens. But it was no different from bringing the animals into the farmhouse during the long Norwegian winter. Now that's something I bet you haven't done – slept with the farm animals!"

"Just Odin," Kaya said. "I like him sleeping next to me in the winter. He's warm."

"We were lucky. Toward the end of the journey it was difficult – bad food, bad water, bad weather, illness, even death." Olena sighed at the memory. "But most of us arrived safely. We all had such high hopes for this new land. And everything our friend had written about America was true. Much of the land is flat and easy to cultivate.

"The weather is so different here. Our first summer here, I feared I would melt from the heat! And it seemed strange at first, being out here with no neighbors for miles around. In Norway, there are people everywhere! But I have grown to love the quiet. There are other Norwegians here a short ride away. And of course our friendly American neighbors."

"Not all Americans are friendly," Kaya said darkly. "*Bestemor*, do you ever wish we were still in Norway? We could all live together, just us Norwegians. We could speak Norwegian all the time, and go to a proper Lutheran church where the pastor was the same every Sunday. No one would make fun of us, or call us Norskies." *And we could be safe from Frank.* A tear leaked out of the corner of Kaya's eye.

"My goodness, child!" Olena said. She pulled a handkerchief from her pocket and dabbed at Kaya's cheek. "Heaven knows there have been some bad times along with the good. The fever took so many, those first years. Then the war was so hard on us all. My Andreas is gone, and your *Onkel* Neil. And now your poor mother. But don't forget the good things here. All of this beautiful land, our freedom, our good neighbors. Lucy, Polly, even little Zachary."

Kaya remembered Frank shoving Zach to the ground. "He did try to help me . . .". Zach didn't say much tonight after they found her. She remembered the blow he took from Frank, and hoped he was all right.

"All in all, I think we made the right decision," Olena continued. "But sometimes I do miss Norway."

Kaya sniffed. "Do you – do you think you will ever go back?" She rubbed her eyes with the heels of her hands, then winced. The bump on her head still hurt.

"An old woman past fifty? No, dear, it is too difficult a journey, much as I would like to go. And the cost! It would take me three or four years' work here on this farm to earn the passage. Oh, no. I think I will stay right here with you." Olena put her handkerchief back in her pocket.

"Please, *Bestemor*, tell me some more," Kaya said. "I'm not a bit tired." An enormous yawn refused to be stifled. She covered her mouth, remembering her manners.

Her grandmother smiled. "Not tired? Come now.

Your eyelids are drooping. Let me tuck you in for the night." She tucked the coverlet around Kaya and smoothed it with both hands.

Kaya looked at her father, no longer pretending but deeply asleep in his chair. "Are you going to tuck Papa in, too?"

"I just might at that." Olena rose and put a hand on Lars' shoulder. He snorted in his chair and came awake. Olena and Kaya exchanged a smile as Lars rose, scratching his belly. He pulled off his boots and tumbled into the other bed.

Kaya's eyelids drooped. She struggled to open them once again. "*Bestemor*, are there any mountains near here?"

"Heavens, no. There are mountains in America, but they are hundreds of miles away from us."

"What about oceans?"

Olena reached out smoothed Kaya's hair gently, careful not to touch the tender bump on her noggin. "Well, you could get to the Gulf of Mexico from here in about a week with a good horse or wagon. I think that is big enough to call an ocean."

"Have you seen it?" Kaya yawned again.

"Yes, when we landed in New Orleans. Do you know where New Orleans is?"

Kaya's eyes were closed now. "Mmmmm," she answered.

"It's in Louisiana. Then we came up the Red River by steamer and took a wagon into Texas. But that is another story."

Olena kissed Kaya lightly on the cheek and blew out the candles before she returned to her own cabin. As she closed the door, darkness settled in. Kaya knew she could not win the battle against sleep and in fact, didn't try. Her last conscious thought was to pat her pocket for her dala horse. It was empty.

CHAPTER TWELVE

The day after the snipe hunt, Kaya woke up with a headache. The bump on her head had started turning colors overnight. As the days passed, the bump slowly improved. Now, four days later, she felt better than it looked. But Kaya had not recovered mentally from being kidnapped by Frank. Frank had made himself clear – he would harm her and her family if she talked about what had happened. Her fear was doubled by having no one to confide in. She considered telling Zach Spence the truth – surely Frank would not harm his own brother? - but he had not been by to see her, and she was too fearful to travel across the prairie alone to visit him at home. Instead, she kept busy around the Olson cabin, never far from her father or grandmother. She only left the cabin to visit the outhouse. Her other chores were either relocated to the cabin or its front porch, or abandoned altogether. Her father was busy in town or on the ranch most days and didn't seem to notice

166

anything was amiss. But she had seen the concerned looks her grandmother gave her.

The quiet days at home since the camp meeting had given Kaya plenty of time to think. She never expected to learn so much information about her mother since coming to Preston. She had more pieces to the puzzle, but just couldn't see how they fit together. And then Frank Spence crossed her path. Frank had handed her some important pieces with one hand, by taking her to meet his father. Then he swept all the pieces off the table when he threatened her and her family. Since the snipe hunt, whenever her thoughts strayed to the puzzle, the memory of Frank's threats swept them away like Odin chasing after scared rabbits. Kaya hated to admit it, but her quest to find answers about her mother's death likely ended on the night of the snipe hunt.

The house was quiet. There was no sign of her father in their half of the cabin. Although she had not breathed a word of her true ordeal with Frank, she could not help but worry for his safety whenever he was away. There was no doubt in her mind that Frank's sarcastic warning about having an 'accident' was a direct reference to what had happened to her grandfather. If she weren't so frightened of Frank, she could tell her father she thought she knew who had killed *Bestefar* Olson, or at least knew something about it. Instead, she kept quiet and spent every day anxiously waiting for his safe return.

She wandered over to her grandmother's side of the cabin. The door was partly open. Inside, Olena sat at the kitchen table peeling potatoes. "*Hallo, Bestemor*," Kaya said.

"*Hallo*, Kaya." Olena put down her knife and wiped her hands. She held a chair out for Kaya. "Have a seat and I will make you something to eat. How is your head feeling?"

"A little better."

"Let's have a look." Her grandmother peered at her carefully. "It is almost back to normal. Soon you will be good as new."

"Is Papa home yet?"

"Yes, Papa is home," Lars called from outside. His boots clunked along the wooden floor. Soon he appeared in the doorway. "I just got back from town. How are you feeling today?" He approached and inspected her bumped head carefully.

"Better, Papa."

"Good." Lars patted Kaya's shoulder gently. He went to the water pitcher and poured some on his hands to wet his face and the back of his neck. "That feels good. It is a hot one today." He wiped his wet hands on the dishtowel hanging nearby, then used it to dry his face. He pulled up a chair at the table and sat down heavily. "*Mor*, you were right, as usual. I finally ran into Sheriff Bradley today. He said a man named Granger was riding shotgun on that wagon that was robbed."

Kaya's stomach clenched at the word 'robbed'. 'Robbed' made her think of bandits, and bandits made her think of Frank. Memories from that night flooded back.

Olena clucked at the news. "I was afraid of that. Have they found the robbers yet?"

Lars shook his head 'no'. "I got the idea he would rather find the wagon. Besides the payroll they were carrying, they had a big shipment of quinine. Doc Medford says fever is going around again. And . . ." Lars hesitated.

Kaya remembered the stack of crates in the corner of the barn.

"And what?" Olena prompted her son to continue. "Kaya?"

Kaya snapped out of her reverie. "Yes, Papa?"

"Kaya, I'm afraid your friend Zach took sick with the fever. That explains why we haven't seen him around lately. *Mor*, Could you stop by there tomorrow?"

"Of course! But what about Kaya? I don't want to leave her alone, especially if she is not feeling well."

"I stopped by the Whitney place on the way home tonight. John said Zelphia and the boys could come over and spend the day with Kaya."

"Papa, how do you spell 'quinine'?" Kaya said.

"What?"

"Quinine. The medicine. How do you spell it?"

"Q-U-I-N-"

"I-N-E?" Kaya finished.

"Yes. Why?"

"It's a funny word. Just wondering." Kaya slumped against the back of her chair.

"For heaven's sake, Kaya. What's wrong? Is it your head?" Olena said.

"No, *Bestemor*," Kaya answered quickly. "I am just thinking about Zach." *And the abandoned graveyard with the fever victims. And the quinine. And Frank.* Kaya remembered Zach's grim description of the horrible disease. "You said there's no quinine. Will Zach get better without the quinine?"

Lars and Olena exchanged a look. He reached across the table but evaded her question. "He is a strong fellow."

Olena said, "Like your father says, Kaya - Zach is a strong boy. His mother and grandmother will take good care of him. I will go over myself soon, and see if there is anything I can do."

"Can I come? I never got a chance to thank him for trying to help me that night."

"Absolutely not," Lars answered. "Kaya, you are not to go over there as long as Zach is sick. I don't want to take any chances of you getting sick, too, especially when there is no quinine."

"Papa - what would happen to those robbers if the sheriff caught them?"

"Jail, then a trial. If they are found guilty of Granger's murder, most likely they would hang."

Ever since Kaya learned about Zach's illness, finding a way to help him was all she could think about. Zach needed quinine. But according to Doc Medford, there wasn't any to be found since the shipment was lost.

Kaya knew differently. She remembered the crates she saw the night Frank brought her to meet Jesse Spence. If she told her father about the quinine, she would have to tell the truth about that night. They would most likely tell Sheriff Bradley. Kaya feared Frank, but he was Zach's brother. She wasn't sure she wanted to be responsible for sending him to jail, or worse. If she didn't tell her father about the quinine, her only other option was to get it herself. Even if she could find that old barn again, and there was still some quinine there, Frank might still be lurking around. Kaya wasn't sure what he would do if he found her there, and she didn't want to find out. She remembered her father's advice they day they went to Preston: 'avoid foolish choices'.

But Kaya felt she had only one choice, foolish or not. She couldn't get the little abandoned graveyard in the woods out of her head: row after row of headstones, many of them dead from the fever. Kaya didn't blame Zach for what happened with Frank. She hadn't known Zach long, but she couldn't help but like him. Having a friend felt good - much better than feeling guilty.

Feeling guilty was new to Kaya. She didn't like it. Even though her father had assured her she was not responsible for her mother's death, that didn't make her feel any better. She would give anything to have that day back, to do things differently, to not have their quarrel possibly be the reason her mother left. It was too late to do anything about her mother. But it wasn't too late for Zach. Kaya wanted to make the right choices. She knew where to find some quinine. If she didn't help Zach, and he died from the fever, she could never forgive herself.

Her plan was simple: she would ride Dala back to that barn and get the quinine. It was time she started riding again. If she could find the barn, get the medicine and get back before she was missed, everything would be fine. She wasn't sure how she would explain to her father. She would worry about that when the time came.

Kaya got up quietly. Her father snored lightly as she passed by his bed and out their front door. She made her way down the narrow passageway between their cabin and her grandmother's. Locusts buzzed in the warm night air. Kaya entered the barn through the small door and found her way to the horses. Old Ned and Dala stood in adjacent stalls side by side, quiet but aware of her approach. Kaya checked the tack in the dim light to confirm her mother's small saddle was still hanging where she had last seen it. One of the milking stools should work for her to get the saddle on Dala. She dipped into the carrot basket and fed one to each. "I'm sorry, girl," she said to Dala. "When I see you, I think of Mama, and that makes me sad to ride you. But I can't be sad tomorrow." Kaya hoped she had the courage to do what must be done.

CHAPTER THIRTEEN

The next morning Kaya got up and got dressed. She had a plan for getting the quinine for Zach, but much could go wrong.

Her heart pounded as she opened the door to her grandmother's cabin. Olena was stirring the coals at her hearth. "Kaya! My goodness. What are you doing up so early? I was just about to make your breakfast."

"I couldn't sleep, *Bestemor.*" *At least that much was true.* "Can I help?"

"Are you sure you are up to it?"

"Yes, *Bestemor.* I feel better today." Kaya avoided her grandmother's eyes.

"Thank you, Kaya. Could you bring in the eggs? I don't know how I ever got along without you. You are a treasure."

Kaya swallowed hard. *I hope you feel the same way when I see you again tonight.*

Kaya stood on the cabin porch with the egg basket in her hand, peering into the predawn gloom. Her skin crawled. She imagined Frank appearing from out of nowhere, sweeping down on her from his horse to carry her away again. She took a deep breath, exhaled, and walked across the front yard, fighting the urge to turn and look behind her.

The chickens clucked quietly inside the hen house. Kaya gathered the eggs quickly. Instead of returning to her grandmother's kitchen, she entered the barn and set down her basket. "All right, Dala, today's the day I start riding you again."

Kaya stopped in front of Dala's stall. It was empty. "Where is she?" Kaya said to no one. "Where's Dala?" Old Ned stuck his head out of his stall to see what the fuss was about. He shook his head and snorted, hoping for another carrot. Kaya checked the other stalls, but they were empty also. She checked the corral. Heart pounding, she raced back to her grandmother's cabin.

"*Bestemor*!"

"Yes, dear? What's wrong?"

"It's bandits! They took Dala!"

176

"What? Oh, no dear, Dala is fine. Here, have a seat. Mind your head. You shouldn't get yourself so worked up." Olena urged Kaya toward a chair.

"But, *Bestemor* – where is she?"

"Your papa rode Dala into town to work today so I can take the wagon to the Spences. He didn't want me walking in this heat. And she hasn't been ridden since you two arrived. He thought she might enjoy a little exercise."

Kaya sat down heavily. "He took Dala?"

"Yes, dear. Why?"

"Nothing, *Bestemor*."

"Kaya, isn't there something you're forgetting?"

Kaya stared at her grandmother mutely.

"Were there any eggs today?"

"Eggs? Oh. Yes. I must have . . . I'll be right back." Her grandmother eyed her closely as she went back out.

As Kaya retrieved the eggs, her mind was spinning. No Dala, no trip to the old barn. No trip, no quinine. No quinine, no help for Zach. Now what? She noted the progress of the sun. She tried to guess how long it would take to get to Preston on foot. Kaya made up her mind to continue with her plan. *Just act normal.*

"Lots of eggs today," Kaya said as brightly as she

could, putting the basket on the kitchen table. "Plenty to share with the Spences."

"Spences?"

"Aren't you visiting Zach today? From what Papa said, it sounds like they really need you."

"Well, I want to, but I don't want to leave you here. You seem . . . not quite yourself yet." Olena reached out to check Kaya's head.

Kaya willed herself not to flinch. "I'm better, *Bestemor*. Don't worry about me. Odin and I will be fine. Zelphia will drop by, like Papa said. It sounds like Zach needs you more than I do. "

"Your father did make it sound as if I should go as soon as I could. . . well, I suppose if you are feeling well enough . . . Let's have some breakfast, and then I will head over. But not for long! I will be back before suppertime."

Kaya choked down her fried eggs and milk into her clenching stomach as if it were the best meal of her life. She did not want to give her grandmother any reason to cancel her trip to the Spence's. At last they finished. As Olena reached for her apron, Kaya reached for it and said, "I'll do the dishes, *Bestemor.*" Olena raised an eyebrow, but handed her apron over. "Would you like some help

178

hitching Old Ned?" Kaya asked.

"Why, yes, I suppose . . ." Olena answered as Kaya led the way to the barn. Working together, they soon had the wagon ready to go. At last, she waved good-bye to Kaya and headed out of the yard and onto the open prairie.

Kaya waved back as her grandmother turned around not once, but twice to look at her. After she disappeared into the distance, Kaya counted slowly to one hundred. Then she repeated the process in English to be sure her grandmother did not return for some forgotten item or with a change of heart. Finally, she went to the desk near her grandmother's bed and retrieved a sheet of paper, a pen, and the ink bottle.

Dear Zelphia,
Kaya is feeling much better today so I took her with
me to the Spences.
Here are some eggs for your trouble.
Olena Olson

Kaya hoped Zelphia wouldn't notice it wasn't Olena's handwriting. She placed the note in the middle of the kitchen table under a basket containing a few eggs her grandmother had left behind. Kaya regretted having Zelphia walk over again today, only to turn around and go back home – or at least Kaya hoped she would. She went back to their side of the cabin to see if there was anything there she might need on her journey. Nothing else seemed of any use. With one last check to make sure the coast was clear, Kaya stepped out the front door and almost stepped on Odin. Odin raised his head to see what she was up to. "It's okay, boy. Go back to your nap." As trustful as her grandmother, Odin did as he was told.

As she hurried along, Kaya calculated her path over and over again. The Olson place was on the edge of the big prairie east of Preston. Kaya remembered her grandmother saying her cabin was about three miles from town. She knew she had to head toward Preston to find the place where the camp meeting had been held. A brisk wind lifted her bonnet's ribbons. Menacing slate-gray clouds lined the western horizon. Kaya told herself it was the rising sun at her back that made them seem so dark.

Thinking back to the night of the camp meeting, Kaya remembered as they headed into the setting sun, they had turned off the road to the right to arrive at the camp site. Thanks to her father's lengthy instruction about the four compass directions during their move to Preston, she knew turning right facing the setting sun meant they were heading north. Today the sun was closer to rising than to setting. But Kaya knew the sun traveled east to west. She knew where it would set. So as long as she kept it behind her during the morning, she knew she would eventually need to turn right to find the camp site. Kaya also tried to account for the difference in the time it would take to get there. That night they had been in the wagon, but today she was on foot.

Human voices soon interrupted the tweets and rustles of nature. Kaya ducked behind a scrawny mesquite tree, wishing it was bigger, and peered around it. Zelphia Whitney and her two young sons approached from the west, not 30 paces distant. Zelphia had a basket on one arm and the youngest boy by the hand. The older boy darted among the trees running ahead, then back as his mother urged him to stay within sight. Kaya hoped her forged note was good enough to convince Zelphia everything was fine and she could return home without raising an alarm.

Kaya waited until the Whitneys passed her. Then she crept in the opposite direction from tree to shrub, blocking herself from their view. At last they distanced themselves far enough away that she dared moving in an upright stance again. Seeing the Whitneys reminded her that she hadn't seen the Whitney cabin on the way to the camp meeting that night. They must have passed by it before turning right. So she did the same - she waited until the Whitney place came into view before turning north.

The sun was above the treetops by the time she reached the site of the camp meeting. Kaya's heart nearly burst with relief at finding it. The location was obvious. Wagon ruts and flattened grass still marked the spot nearly a week later. Kaya took some time to get her bearings and find the area where she and the other children had played hide and seek in the woods. Where Frank found them.

Now what? She didn't think Frank would have come from the direction of town (west). If he was hiding out, he likely would have avoided the camp meeting and all those people (east of town), so she ruled out those directions. That left north and south. Kaya noticed the woods began to thin out sooner to the north. The barn had been on open ground, not in the woods, so she headed in that direction. She found an animal trail, a narrow path ever so slightly beaten into the earth. Following the trail, she kept the sun to her right and hoped she had chosen correctly.

Sturdy oaks and pecans eventually gave way to a few gangly mesquite trees. Kaya trudged along. Her mind had exhausted itself with plots and plans and counter-plans. It now focused on more basic tasks, like walking in a straight line. Her head ached. Her legs ached. Her shoes rubbed her feet. Her throat was parched. When the sun was not behind a cloud, it was almost directly overhead. Kaya knew this meant it was near lunch time. She guessed she had been walking for about two hours. By now Zelphia had certainly reached the Olson place. If her note hadn't worked, someone was probably out looking for her by now.

The prairie landscape varied so little, Kaya feared the faint trail was leading her in circles. She was ready to admit defeat and get back home before she got herself into deeper trouble. But something kept her from turning around. *You've come this far. Don't give up now.* She made a bargain with herself: just 100 more steps. If she hadn't made any progress finding the barn after 100 steps, she'd turn around.

So Kaya stuck with the trail. At Step 89, it lead her to a small plateau with a view of the prairie beyond. And just like that, there it was: a ramshackle barn stood no more than a quarter mile away. There was only one problem - the barn sat in the middle of the open prairie. She had a quarter mile to go, with little to hide her approach.

The heavy clouds that lined the western horizon when she began her journey were now directly overhead. Lighter wisps dangled lower here and there, threatening rain. She could smell it in the air. Kaya sat with her back next to one of the scrappy mesquite trees on the edge of the woods and scanned the prairie for human activity. There was none. She stalled as long as she dared, screwing up her courage. But she could not afford to wait any longer.

An old feed shed crouched near the barn. Kaya ran for it. She crossed the prairie, legs pumping, before collapsing into the hay and dried cow patties beneath the shed. She tried to quiet her breathing, expecting Frank or one of his gang to charge out after her at any moment. She squeezed under the feed trough and eyed the barn. The wind ruffled the prairie grasses, but otherwise, it was completely silent. A stone chimney stood alone in the prairie on the far side of the barn. Debris littered the grass – a lone fence post broken in half, a rusted plow half buried in the ground, chunks of charred wood.

Kaya chose her moment and raced into the gaping entrance of the barn. It was shady and smelled like every barn in the world, of hay and animals and manure. Nothing stirred. That night, the crates, bags, and Frank's father had been in a corner of the barn. There was nothing here now, no sign of them. But it had been dark, and she had been blindfolded. Maybe they had come in the opposite end of the barn. She tiptoed down the length of the barn, avoiding piles of manure.

At the other end of the barn she came to the last stall. To her right something caught her eye. There! In the gloomy corner, dust motes floating in the air above, sat a single crate. One corner was bashed in. Kaya hurried over. Brown glass littered the hay near the crate. "Please," she whispered, squatting to pick through the debris.

BANG!

Kaya shot up and squealed in spite of herself.

BANG!

The small entry door at her end of the barn flapped against the outside wall. Outside the wind had picked up. Thunder rumbled in the distance. Kaya returned to the crate, the barn door flapping and banging occasionally as she pawed through the debris with trembling hands.

Three precious bottles of quinine had survived inside the damaged crate. *Please let it be enough.* She put one in each apron pocket and carried the third in one hand.

Rain began to pepper the roof and the parched ground outside. It fell gently at first, then more urgently. Kaya jumped as lightning flashed, quickly followed by a crack of thunder. The wind howled through the openings in the barn's upper story.

Kaya stood up and turned to leave. Two steps from the crate, she stepped on something hard underfoot. Thinking it might be another bottle of quinine, she knelt and felt for it. She dug it out of the ground with some effort - apparently she was not the first to have stepped on it. Encrusted with dirt, but still in one piece, lay her dala horse.

Kaya stared. Instantly she thought of her mother and how she had cherished it so. "It's special," she always said to Kaya when Kaya wanted to play with it. "Be careful."

"Now look at you," she said as she picked it up. She rubbed off some of the dirt onto her now filthy apron.

"Yes, just look at you."

CHAPTER FOURTEEN

Kaya wheeled around. Frank Spence stood halfway down the barn, nothing but a black shadow with the gray storm light behind him. "I thought you said you were a smart girl." He walked toward her, weaving slightly. "Maybe too smart."

Kaya stood petrified, dala horse in one hand, a bottle of quinine in the other. As Frank approached, she smelled something sour, medicinal. A large clear bottle dangled from his hand, half full of copper-colored liquid. Raindrops dripping from his hat darkened his faded red shirt.

"Please," she croaked, backing away. "I only came for the quinine. Zach is sick."

"Zach?" Frank frowned. He stumbled backwards a step and caught himself clumsily.

"Your brother, Zach."

"Hmmph. Brother. Little tadpole," Frank mumbled.

187

He took a long pull from the bottle, then stared at Kaya for a moment with bloodshot eyes. "He's dead now. It's all your fault."

"Dead! No!" *All of this for nothing.* "But – he can't be dead! He 's sick, but he was alive, yesterday." Tears filled her eyes.

Frank snorted. "Yesterday? He's been cold in the grave for three days. You're as crazy as he was, at the end."

Kaya took another careful step back from Frank. He didn't seem to notice. He wiped his mouth on his shirtsleeve. "*Who's* dead, Frank?"

"My pa. Who'd ya think? Deader'n dead. That bullet in his gut did him in. He had a fever and talked crazy all night. Then he died. Like that." Frank attempted a clumsy snap with his free hand. "Babbling one minute, dead the next."

Kaya recalled Jesse Spence, with his wild hair and piercing eyes. "I- I'm sorry."

Frank's head snapped up. "You should be. Your ma got him killed. If it weren't for him bug-wild to get to her, he'd be alive right now. 'One more job, Frank,' he said, 'One more big score and I'm going to take my Alma away

188

for good.'"

Kaya stared at Frank open-mouthed, halting her stealthy retreat.

Frank peered at Kaya. "You didn't know, did you? Nobody did, 'cept me. Pa trusted me. He and your ma had been runnin' off together for years. A day or two here, a week there. She put one over on your pa all these years. She was a slick one, your ma."

"Shut up about my mama!" Kaya said. "It's not true! Mama loved Papa!"

"So your ma never left home now and then? Maybe she said she was visiting relatives?" Frank asked, wiggling his eyebrows. Kaya hated his smarmy tone. She hated even worse that he was right.

"She was visiting, all right, but 'tweren't no relatives." Frank chuckled at his joke. His laugh died when he saw Kaya's face. He cleared his throat and said, "Where is she, anyway? All Pa could say, at the end, was 'Where's Alma? Where's Alma?' He went to all that trouble, got hisself shot, and she didn't even bother to show up and meet him. We waited in the thicket at Cedar Creek for three days and nights, Pa needing a doctor but refusing to leave, waiting for his Alma. If we had got him to a doctor .

. . ."

Kaya shook her head, refusing to believe this drunken bully. "You're wrong. Mama died on the way to visit *Bestemor*. Bandits robbed her stage coach. She got shot."

"Stage coach?" Frank repeated. "And where was she going in her stage coach?"

"She was coming to visit *Bestemor*. Grandmother Olson."

"So, she was headed to visit relatives?"

Kaya ground her teeth at the hateful phrase. "Yes."

"In Preston?"

Kaye nodded curtly.

"Which happens to be where my Pa lived," Frank sneered. "She was shot during a stage coach robbery? When was this?"

"August 3," Kaya answered. In all that had happened, that was one thing she was sure of.

Frank shook his head. "I'll be damned. Stage coach between Hillsboro and Corsicana?"

Kaya nodded again. "Wait - how do you know -" then she stopped as realization struck. "It was *you*. You and your . . . gang. *You* killed my mama." Kaya shivered as a chill ran down her back.

"Whoa, now, girlie, not true, not true! It was that shotgun rider what did it." Frank sagged down onto a bale of hay. He rested his elbows on his knees and put his head in his hands. Finally, he looked up. "No wonder she never showed up. Being dead and all."

"So it *was* your gang?"

"I guess it was. We heard there was a big payroll shipment coming by stage from Austin to Dallas. Their stage broke down, so they transferred the strong box to a different stage in Hillsboro. Unmarked."

"How did you know?"

"Let's just say the blacksmith in Austin owed Pa a favor. The breakdown weren't exactly an accident." Frank sighed and dusted hay off his pants. The last few days had taken their toll. In the filtered daylight inside the barn, he seemed less a fierce bandit and more a tired young man, old before his time. "We trailed 'em out of Hillsboro, looking for our chance. We thought we caught a piece of luck when that dern fool guard stopped the wagon to track down a turkey he shot. But the strong box was bolted in but good - was the devil to get out. While we were foolin' with that, the guard and his new Henry rifle came up on us from behind. He drew down on us, told us to git. We didn't. Pa took a shot at him. He shot back. And I guess you know the rest. His shot went clean through Pa - "

"And hit Mama," Kaya finished.

"-and hit somebody in the stage," Frank nodded. "We didn't know who, just heard a ruckus, which we were glad of – gave us a chance to hightail it out of there. So that was your ma got shot?"

Kaya nodded.

"What was she doing on the stage? She usually rode that little sorrel of hers - Dilly, Dolly. . ."

"Dala."

"Huh?"

"Her horse. Her name is Dala." Frank's question hung in the air. Why the stage? Then Kaya remembered Sheriff Taylor returning her mother's trunk from that fateful stage trip, filled with everything she held dear. Her heart sank.

Frank seemed not to notice Kaya's silent musings. "The two of them, killed by the same man, hell, the same bullet even," he continued. "It's a good thing Pa died before he found this out. He woulda hunted that guard down for sure for killing his Alma."

Kaya's hands clenched, digging her nails into her palms. "It's *your* fault," she blurted, eyes blazing. "If you hadn't robbed that stage, my mama would still be alive."

Frank snorted. "*My* fault? If your mama hadn't been cheatin' on your pa, runnin' off with *my* pa, she wouldn't a been on that stage in the first place. *My* fault. *Hmmpf!*"

"She didn't! She wasn't! Take it back!"

Frank cocked an eyebrow and let Kaya think.

Another bolt of lightning struck nearby and Kaya flinched. Frank remained unaffected by the storm swirling around them. Thunder crashed, and he shook his head like Odin shaking off water. His eyes cleared. He stood up and cleared his throat. "Who knows you're here?"

"No one. I didn't tell anyone. Honest."

"No one? You came out here all by yourself? Ain't no way a little girl like you didn't have some help finding this place."

Kaya shook her head. "No! Zach's sick. He needs the quinine. I saw it here that night. I hoped there was some left. I just – walked until I found it." Frank took a step closer and she took another step back. "Let me go. I haven't said a word to anyone, and I still won't. Zach needs the quinine. He might – he might die."

"Sorry, kid. Can't do that." Frank lunged for Kaya, grabbing at her with his empty hand. Kaya smashed him in the face with the bottle of quinine she still held. It shattered and the liquid burst all over both of them. Frank yelled and grabbed his injured face. He stumbled and fell backwards over a bale of hay, striking his head against one of the stalls. As he lay there moaning, Kaya turned and tore out of the barn. *If I can make it to the woods, maybe I have a chance.*

Once outside Kaya was immediately drenched by the raging storm. Angry fat drops blew into her sideways, driven by the wind. Behind her, a horse whinnied. She turned to see if somehow Frank had already recovered from his fall and was riding down on her. But it was only his horse, Dagger, standing under the feed shed where she had hidden earlier. He seemed unconcerned about the storm. His reins dragged loosely along the ground.

Kaya checked again for any sign of Frank. Her heart sank. He had stumbled to the barn door and was shaking his head again to clear his vision. A streak of blood ran from his temple, diluted by the rain. She made her decision. As she charged towards Dagger, Frank shouted.

Once under the feed shed, Kaya hopped on the

194

edge of the wooden trough and reached for Dagger's saddle horn. Her fear gave her an extra boost as she clawed her way up the rigging. Still clutching her dala horse in one hand, she shoved it into her pocket, scratched madly for Dagger's reins and righted herself. Pulling equally on both reins, she backed Dagger out of the shed and turned him around. As she had seen Frank do, she yelled "Yah! Yah!" and gave Dagger two firm heels to the ribs. Dagger bolted, throwing Kaya back in the saddle. She clung to the reins for dear life, slipping sideways in the saddle. They were on a collision course with Frank now, who was shouting at his horse and waving his arms in the air. "Come on, boy," she said. She jerked Dagger's reins to the left and they made an awkward circle around Frank, just out of his reach. Kicking up clods of mud, Kaya and Dagger headed for the woods. Kaya didn't look back.

CHAPTER FIFTEEN

Kaya rode Dagger back the way she came as quickly as she could without knocking herself out of the saddle on some low-hanging branch. Dagger was patient with her, considering she hadn't ridden a horse lately. He slipped once, pitching her backwards. She caught herself with the reins. "Sorry, boy," she said after accidentally jerking him to a halt.

They followed the trail in fits and starts until they finally lost sight of Frank, and Kaya relaxed enough to let Dagger set the pace. The storm clouds blotted out the sun, so she kept the animal trail in sight as best she could in the driving rain to keep from getting lost. But she had a hard time focusing on the trail. All she could think about was what she had learned from Frank Spence.

Was it true - her mother died on the way to run off with Jesse Spence? So many of her questions about her mother's death had now been answered. Alma Olson had claimed to be headed to visit an ailing *Bestemor* Olson who had not been sick in years, who lived in a town which also happened to be where Jesse Spence lived. She took the stage with all of her worldly belongings, rather than riding her favorite horse. Frank and Jesse Spence certainly seemed to know her mother, and even knew of Kaya. Frank knew the details of the stage robbery that killed her mother. But Frank was a bandit, a criminal, and likely a liar to boot. Kaya didn't know why he would lie to her about her mother's death. But she wouldn't put it past him. She didn't know what to believe.

When Kaya reached the prairie where the camp meeting had been held, she turned north toward the Spence cabin. She had been so wrapped up in her escape, she forgot to be afraid of Dagger. She knew her destination now, so she let Dagger travel as fast as she dared. At last, the trees thinned. Kaya sighted the cabin ahead. The Olson wagon was out front. Old Ned and Dala nibbled nearby, seeking shelter from the light rain under a large live oak.

Kaya wheeled into the front yard of the Spence place and slid sideways off Dagger. His sides were slick with rain and sweat. "Good boy, Dagger. I'll be right back to give you a drink." She looped his reins lightly around one of the front porch railings. He snorted and backed away from Kaya, then nibbled at some long grass sprouting around an old half barrel full of yarrow. "Where were you this morning when I needed you?" Kaya called out to Dala. Dala looked up and twitched an ear toward Kaya, then returned to her own grazing.

Kaya dashed onto the porch and through the open door. "Mrs. Spence, I —"

Four heads turned to see what the commotion was. Lucy Spence sat next to the bed in the corner, holding Zach's hand as he lay quietly. His face was pale, his wild hair damp from fever sweat. Polly Spence sat in her rocker near the hearth, clutching her cane in front of her. Olena Olson stood at the end of the bed. She was wringing out a wet cloth into a porcelain bowl on the dresser, but stopped when Kaya burst in. "Kaya?" Lars Olson stepped out of the shadows near Zach's bed. "What are you doing here? You shouldn't be here. And where have you been? You're soaking wet!"

"Good heavens, child!" her grandmother said. "You're a mess!"

Kaya didn't answer her father. She approached

Lucy Spence and held out the two small brown bottles. "Quinine," Kaya said. "For Zach."

"Quinine-" Lucy breathed. She read the labels. "It *is* quinine. But . . . how?"

"It's not important," Kaya said. "Just give it to him. Please, ma'am?"

Lucy nodded. She put one of the bottles in her pocket and uncorked the other. Gently lifting Zach's head, she tipped some into his mouth. He groaned, but his eyes never opened. After he swallowed, she tipped a little more, then lay his head back down. His eyes fluttered open. Kaya wasn't sure he was well enough to recognize her - until he smiled weakly and wheezed, "Norskie," then closed his eyes again.

Kaya exhaled the breath she didn't realize she had been holding and walked back into the kitchen area. Water dripped off her and onto the floor. Her right hand began to throb. It was red with blood. Her blood. Then she remembered – the quinine bottle she had broken into Frank's face. "Hunh," she said and sat down clumsily on the wooden floor.

"Kaya!" Her father and grandmother rushed to her side. "Let me see that," her grandmother said. Kaya sat numbly, suddenly exhausted. Her dress stuck wetly to her legs and back. Her soaked bonnet sagged heavily down her back, choking her with its tied ribbons. She pulled it up and over her head with her good hand.

Olena wiped away the blood and inspected her wound. "What happened, Kaya?"

"Broke one of the bottles. I had three but one of them. . . broke."

Olena retrieved her basket of medical supplies from Zach's bedside and found some cotton fabric. She ripped it neatly lengthwise and began winding it around Kaya's palm. "How is that, dear?"

Kaya nodded. "Fine, *Bestemor*. Thank you."

"Kaya, what is this all about?," her father said. "What are you doing here, soaking wet? Where did you get the quinine?"

"Where did I get it?" Kaya snapped out of her daze. *Frank.* Frank would surely track her down. And he knew how to get here, here of all places. She tried to stand up. Her father held out his hand to help her. "We have to leave, Papa. It's not safe here. We have to get Sheriff Bradley. Please, Papa!" Kaya gripped her father's arm with her bandaged hand as best she could. She pulled him toward the door.

"Hush, girl! Come over here so we don't disturb Zach." He steered Kaya back to the kitchen table and sat her down. He switched to Norwegian. "Now listen to me, young lady. We're not going anywhere until you tell me what happened." He took the chair next to her and turned it so that he was facing her. "What are you talking about?" he asked quietly. "What's this about the sheriff?"

Kaya's resolve faltered under the weight of her father's caring look. "Frank, Papa. He'll track me down."

Lucy glanced toward Lars at the mention of Frank, but stayed where she was. Polly Spence rose from her rocking chair and joined the group at the table.

"Frank!" Lars hissed, lowering his voice. His eyes darted toward the front windows of the cabin. "What does he have to do with this? Have you seen him? Did he hurt you? Did he do this?" He reached for her bandaged hand.

"Well, no. I did it. I smashed him in the face with a bottle of quinine and it broke."

"*What*? When?"

"A little while ago, Papa. Just before I came here."

Lars shook his head. "Tell me everything. From the beginning."

Polly Spence dragged her rocker closer to the table and sat. "In English, please?"

Lars frowned, then nodded once to Kaya.

Kaya did as she was told. She started with the night Frank kidnapped her. She told of the boxes of quinine she saw there. "That's where I went, Papa, to get the quinine for Zach. But Frank was there. He was awful mad. He might have followed me back here."

"How far away is this barn, Kaya?"

Kaya tried to explain where it was. Lars nodded. "The old Carson place, I expect."

Polly Spence nodded. "Yes, there was a fire several years ago. That's the only fire I know of in these parts."

"But that's all the way over to Neals Prairie. How did you get there and back so quickly?"

Dagger. She had forgotten all about the horse. "I walked there this morning, after *Bestemor* left to visit Zach. After, I took Frank's horse and rode him back here." She stood up. "He needs a drink."

Her father stopped her with a gentle hand on her shoulder and sat her back down. "This morning - but didn't Zelphia -"

"I left before she got there. I wrote her a note like I

202

was *Bestemor* and told her we changed our plans and she could go back home."

Lars ran a hand through his hair. "Sneaking out, stealing horses, forgery – what's next, a bank robbery?" He tried to look stern, but softened at the sight of Kaya slumped in her chair. "If you took his horse, he's on foot at least. That's a good thing. We won't be seeing him too soon, I think."

"I don't know, Papa. Frank has a habit of turning up."

"Don't worry, Kaya. You're safe now." He stood and said, "You stay put. I'll see to the horse."

"And I think that's enough excitement for one day," Olena said as her son went outside. She helped Kaya out of her chair. "Thanks to the quinine, I think we can leave Zachary in the care of these two ladies. Let's get you home and into some dry clothes."

"Wait, *Bestemor*. There's something else. It's important." Kaya looked to her grandmother, then Polly Spence. "Mrs. Spence, I'm so sorry," she began.

"Why, whatever for, dear?"

"Frank's father –"

"Jesse?" she asked eagerly. "Have you seen him?

Do you know where he is?"

"Yes, I – I saw him that night. When Frank took me. I think that's why he took me. To see his father."

"To see Jesse?"

"Yes, Jesse," Kaya continued. She had to know. "Jesse – Mr. Spence - said he knew my mama." She turned to her grandmother. "Is that right, *Bestemor*? Did Mr. Spence know Mama?"

Before Olena could answer, Polly said, "Yes, dear, of course he did. But tell me – where is my Jesse?"

Kaya didn't know what else to say. "He's dead, ma'am," she said quietly. She glanced at Lucy Spence, but Lucy was wiping Zach's forehead and appeared not to have heard. "Frank said he was dead."

"Dead!" Polly Spence exclaimed. "No!" Her exclamation got Lucy's attention. She tucked the quilt under Zach's chin and quietly joined them.

"What's wrong?" she whispered, looking from Polly to Olena to Kaya. "What's all this fuss about?"

Polly Spence wept into her apron. "Jesse's dead!" she managed, before choking out more sobs.

"Dead!" Lucy gasped, her hand flying to her mouth as if trying, too late, to prevent that word from emerging.

Olena repeated Kaya's story to Lucy quickly and quietly. She blinked rapidly and turned to comfort her mother-in-law.

"What's that you have, dear?" Olena asked Kaya. "More quinine?"

Kaya followed her grandmother's gaze to her own hand, clenched around the dala horse in her pocket. She relaxed her fingers. "No, it's Mama's dala horse. I lost it that night, but I found it in the barn today." She began rubbing off the grime of the barn with a corner of her apron. As she wiped it clean, some of the dirt remained imbedded into a small carving on its belly. It stood out starkly against the white paint. Kaya stopped wiping. Her mouth went dry. The carving was in the shape of an S. She remembered Frank's words in the barn. She remembered the wounded man, Jesse, and how he seemed to know her mother. Then she recalled her mother's words the first time she showed Kaya the horse.

Kaya returned to Polly Spence and patted her on the arm. Without saying a word, Kaya held out the horse.

Polly took it from her and immediately turned it over. There was no mistaking the S on its stomach. "Where did you get this?" Polly sniffed.

"It was my mother's. I found it in her trunk."

"Did she tell you where she got it?"

Kaya remembered the first time she saw the dala horse. She was sitting in the sun on a blue and white rag rug in their living room in the house in Normandy, playing at her mother's feet. The horse fell out of her mother's pocket. Alma reached for it, but Kaya got it first. As she handed it back to her mother's outstretched hand, she felt the little nubs for ears atop its head; the curve of its neck; its tan, painted-on saddle. Delicate bright blue lines curving along its reins and halter. Kaya had been in love with it ever since. "She said . . . she said her *kjære* made it for her," Kaya answered.

"*Shada?*"

"Yes - her sweetheart. I thought she meant Papa."

Polly Spence walked over to the bureau and retrieved something from the top drawer. When she returned, she held out her hand. In it was her own dala horse, nearly a twin to Kaya's. She turned it over. There was the S, carved in the same spot. "Yes, dear. Sweetheart. But not your father." She waited to see Kaya's reaction.

Olena stepped in, finally realizing what was happening. "Come, Kaya. Zach could use some peace and

206

quiet." She tried to take Kaya's hand, but Kaya resisted gently. Her eyes never left Polly Spence.

"Are you saying . . . are you saying Mr. Spence and Mama . . . " Kaya asked.

Mrs. Spence smiled through her tears. She stepped toward Kaya. "He loved your mother so much." Mrs. Spence sniffed and dug in her apron pocket, retrieving a crumpled handkerchief. She blew her nose and dabbed at her eyes. "It broke his heart when they sent her away. Never got over it."

"Sent her away? Where did she go?"

"Why, to Normandy, of course." Polly Spence sighed. "It never pays to keep family secrets," she said, darting a look toward Olena. "Somehow they always spill out. Jesse was always fond of pretty girls, and they liked him, too. He was such a rounder, that one, when he was younger. But when Alma Pierson came along, that was it! She was the one for him. They were so much in love. . . "

"I don't believe you!" Kaya said.

Footsteps tread on the front porch. "Now what?" Lars Olson said as he entered. "Is it Zach? Is he all right?"

"Not Zach, Lars," Olena said. "Kaya knows about Alma and Jesse."

"Knows what?"

"Papa?" Kaya's stomach flipped. "It's not true. About Mama and . . . Mr. Spence."

Lars gently took the dala horse from Kaya and noted the S on its belly. "Yes, Kaya, it's true."

CHAPTER SIXTEEN

Kaya dashed past her father and out the front door of the Spence cabin. She was down the steps and into the yard before she stopped. There she just stood in the light drizzle, staring into the empty prairie, seeing nothing. Her thoughts raced in circles around the impossible news that her mother had loved someone other than her father. And that someone was the outlaw Jesse Spence. And she was likely on her way to reunite with Spence when she died.

"Kaya," her grandmother called softly.

Olena closed the front door quietly behind her. "Come out of the rain, dear." Kaya's mind barely registered her grandmother's words, but her feet obeyed. She sat down heavily on the top step. Olena sat down next to her. She took one of Kaya's hands in hers. "I know it is a shock."

Kaya said nothing.

"Your mother and Jesse Spence – well, they were

209

young and I suppose they thought they were in love," Olena continued. "But your mother's parents, the Piersons –*hvil i fred* – were very traditional. They did not approve of Jesse Spence. They were determined that Alma marry a Norwegian. Because we had come to America together, and Lars was not yet married, they asked us to allow Lars to marry Alma. Lars was not happy about it either, as he had someone else in mind for a wife."

Kaya's eyebrows shot up. "Who?"

"Don't you know?"

Kaya sat up. She remembered her father's awkwardness in Mr. Bakken's store, the look on his face as he entered the Spence cabin. Kaya now realized it was not a look of contentment, but of love. "Lucy Spence," Kaya said.

Olena nodded. "Carlisle was her maiden name. Lars thought Lucy Carlisle was the finest girl he had ever seen. But Lars has always been a responsible son, and he did what was asked of him. The Piersons moved to Normandy. They arranged for a place for Lars and your mother to live, to separate her from Jesse Spence. Your *Tante* Julia and *Onkel* Otto moved there also, to keep them company."

"Is that why Mama was never happy? I thought it was because of me."

"Because of you? Why on earth would you think that?"

"Nothing was ever right. My stitches were too big. My letters were too messy. My hair was too curly." Tears leaked down Kaya's cheeks. "The only time Mama was happy was when she was riding Dala."

Lars clattered out onto the porch. He stood hesitantly behind them.

Olena squeezed Kaya's hand and stood. "I want to check on Zachary one last time before we go home. Lars, perhaps you and Kaya have some things to talk about?" She patted his arm as she passed him on the way back inside.

Lars ran a hand through his blond hair and sighed. "It's been quite a day for you, hasn't it?" He took his mother's place on the step next to Kaya. "What would you like to know?"

Kaya had so many questions, it was hard to know where to start. If everything she had learned today was true, Kaya now knew her mother didn't leave Normandy because she was angry with Kaya. But the truth didn't make her feel one bit better. At last, she said, "Mrs. Spence said her son came to Normandy all the time." She glanced at her father. "Did you know that?"

Lars' eyebrows shot up. "No, I didn't."

"Is that where Mama went all those times, when you were away working? To meet Mr. Spence?"

"What are you talking about?" Lars asked.

"Mama used to leave me with *Tante* Julia and *Onkel* Otto sometimes when you were gone. She said she was visiting neighbors." Kaya hesitated. "She wasn't visiting neighbors, was she?"

Lars shook his head. "I don't know, Kaya. It seems your mother kept secrets from both of us."

Kaya didn't know what to think. Everything she knew about her parents and her childhood had been turned upside down. Those nagging questions she had about her mother's death, her parents' childhood in Preston, about Jesse Spence – those questions were being answered one by one. But Kaya truly wished she had never begun to ask them.

"How did Mama do it? How did you, and *Bestemor*, and everyone – how did you keep all those secrets for so long? I only had one secret to keep, about

Frank and the barn that night, and I couldn't even keep it for a little while." Kaya sighed. "Papa?"

"Yes?"

"You and Mama – you never loved each other? You got married because your parents made you?"

"Yes, but that is sometimes how it is done in Norway. Your mother and I had our differences. But we did have one thing in common."

"What was that?" Kaya asked quietly.

"Well, you, of course." Lars answered. "It is true, Kaya, that I loved someone else before I met your mother. But I wouldn't wish anything were different, if it meant I couldn't have you. I was there for your first word – do you remember it?

Kaya shook her head 'no'.

"*Kat*," he said. "Although I don't know why - we never had a cat. And your first dog."

"Odin!" Kaya said. "The best dog ever."

Lars grinned. "Yes, he is." Then her father turned serious. "Kaya, I have watched you grow into a lovely young lady. Any father would be proud to have you as a daughter. I know this is a big shock for you. But life will go on. And we will have no more secrets between us."

"No more secrets," Kaya repeated.

"Good." Lars stood. "Time we went home, Kaya. Let me get the horses."

Kaya's eyes strayed to the live oak tree. "Papa? Can I ride her? Can I ride Dala?"

One eyebrow lifted. "Of course, but - are you ready?"

"Yes, Papa. Let's go home."

Norwegian Phrases

Adjø - goodbye

Bestemor - grandmother

Bestefar - grandfather

Bunad - traditional Norwegian women's dress

Gå - go

God dag - good day

God morgen - good morning

Hallo - hello

Hei - hi

Hund - dog

Hvil i fred - rest in peace

Ja - yes

Kat - cat

Kjære - sweetheart

Kjótboller - meatballs in gravy

Lefse - thin unleavened bread made from potatoes

Lutefisk - dried codfish

Mange takk - thanks very much

Mor - mother

Onkel - uncle

Sandbakkel - shortbread cookie

Syttende Mai - May 17, Norway's Constitution Day

Takk - thanks

Tante - aunt

Vær så god - you're welcome

The Backstory

The Dala Horse is my first foray into writing fiction. When I first started writing, it was an outgrowth of my training as a grad student getting my Master's in history. Writing term papers and eventually, my thesis, came naturally to me. When we started our family, like many stay-at-home-moms, I was eager to find an occupation that would bring in some income yet allow me to keep parenting as my main priority. Writing fit the bill perfectly. I had some articles accepted, then branched out into writing non-fiction books for children - the kind you might find in your child's school library.

Eventually I got the itch to write fiction. I still enjoy the research process, but I thought it would be fun if I could relax a little and not feel the need to footnote every paragraph! My love of history, my background in writing for a young audience, and my interest in the Norwegian branch of my family tree became the perfect storm that resulted in *The Dala Horse.*

A few people have asked me why I have chosen a Swedish invention (the dala horse) to spearhead a Norwegian-themed story. Yes, the dala horse originated in Dalarna, Sweden, hundreds of years ago. As I mention on my website, the charming little toy was a product of expert woodworkers with idle time on their hands spent indoors during the long, dark Scandinavian winters. But as is often the case, cultural traditions have no sense of borders. The tradition spread throughout Scandinavia. The little horses acquired the Norwegian rosemaling style of adornment. The two countries were even united under the same government for almost 100 years (1814-1905) which coincides with the time period Kaya's family immigrated to Texas (in the mid-1800s). Kaya's father and grandfather, like many Norwegians as well as other Scandinavians, were expert woodworkers. It seemed reasonable to me that they would have been aware of dala horses and might have carved one or two for their children to play with. It also seemed reasonable that Alma, Kaya's mother, might have mentioned them to Jesse Spence, who perhaps carved one to impress his Norwegian girlfriend. So I hope my Swedish fans will allow me this artistic license. You cannot help but love the little horses, whether you are Swedish, Norwegian, or none of the above.

I should also mention what a great inspiration Elise Waerenskjold, 'the lady with the pen', has been on this project. She was one of the first Norwegian immigrants to Texas and was one of its strongest proponents. Her homestead is near land that is still in my family today. I encourage you to read her journals, letters, and the fine biography written of her by Charles Russell. She was an educated and independent woman, unusual in that time and place. Her story influenced *The Dala Horse* in many ways.

Discussion Guide

The Dala Horse is inspired by Norwegian immigrants who, unlike most Scandinavians, rejected settling in Minnesota and Wisconsin and chose Texas instead. They learned of Texas through the writings of Johan Reinert Reiersen, an intrepid traveler eager to promote the new land to his friends and neighbors in Norway. I'm proud to say I descend from two of these early settlers who arrived in Texas in the mid-1800s.

The history of the Norwegians in Texas has been documented by various scholars as referenced in the bibliography. The character of Olena Olson is inspired by Elise Wjaerenskjold, an independent, free-thinking Norwegian woman. She arrived in Texas in 1847 and settled in the Four Mile area in Kaufman and Van Zandt counties. Mrs. 'Vanshaw' (as the Americans pronounced it) was a prolific letter writer. She promoted Texas in Norway via letters as well as newspaper articles. She was something of a community resource, well informed and respected.

The story takes place in two fictional towns inspired by real communities. It begins in Normandy, a town in Bosque County. I had the community of Norse in mind when I wrote about this town, but I named it Normandy after the original name of Brownsboro, the first Norse community in Texas. Later in the story, Kaya and her father return to his hometown of Preston which is inspired by another Norwegian community, Prairieville in Kaufman County.

As I researched the book, I came across so many interesting facts that stimulated my imagination. Here are a few I thought you would like to know.

Customs

When people move to a new area, they bring their

culture with them. It may be in the form of their language, holidays, clothing, food, or many other things.

- Kaya's mother's trunk, as well as her dala horse, are painted in the Norwegian style known as rosemaling. Rosemaling is a very precise form of decorating objects. It usually includes two or more colors of swirling lines accented with Dala horses originated as children's toys in Sweden. Originally they were plain wood. Eventually they became painted and decorated, often with rosemaling. Today's dala horses can be found in a variety of styles, sizes and colors.

- Porridge, lefse and lutefisk are foods originating in Scandinavia. Porridge is a hot, creamy souplike cereal usually served for breakfast. Lefse is similar to a tortilla but is made from potatoes rather than corn. Lutefisk is fish that has been preserved, or dried, to last throughout the long Scandinavian winters. Lefse and lutefisk are often served as part of the winter holiday meal.

- The Syttende Mai celebration is mentioned twice in this story. Held on May 17, it is the Norwegian version of our July 4 holiday.

Discuss: *What are some things you enjoy that may have come from a different culture?*

Early Texas Newspapers

Newspapers were an important means of communication in the 1800s. Like many aspects of everyday life, Texas newspapers were interrupted by the Civil War but sprang back quickly after it ended. By the late 1860s several papers were in circulation in East Texas. Publication schedules varied. News traveled much more slowly then. Newspaper delivery was by horse (wagon, stage coach) and later by train and therefore delayed by days, weeks, or longer.

Discuss: *Imagine life today without instant access to news – no phones, TVs, or Internet. How would you find out what was going on in your school? Family? Neighborhood? Town?*

Sharecroppers

Sharecropping became common in the American south after the Civil War. With the end of slavery after the war, many landholders suddenly had no one to work their land. And there was an excess of laborers due to the elimination of slavery. So they used a system of sharecropping to meet both needs. It worked like this: landowners made a deal with workers to farm their land. In exchange, they shared a set amount of the profits or products (usually half) with the workers. Many freed slaves became sharecroppers after.

Discuss: *Do you have any projects that you need help with? What would you be willing to trade to help get the* *work done?*

Stagecoaches

Texas stagecoaches had their roots in the early days of the Republic of Texas. Routes grew with the population. By the 1860s there were dozens of routes crisscrossing Texas, carrying not only people but mail and freight. They provided a valuable and affordable service in an era before cars, trains, and airplanes.

Coaches were large enclosed carriages pulled buy several horses or mules. The 'horsepower' was replaced with fresh animals at various stops or 'stages' along the route so the coach could continue rolling throughout the daylight hours. The coaches were not heated or air conditioned. They averaged around 60 miles per day. Old routes often became the paved highways we still travel today.

Discuss: *Although transportation technology has improved* *since the time of this story, we still sometimes find ourselves traveling in uncomfortable circumstances. What are some things that make traveling more comfortable and enjoyable for you? What makes it unpleasant?*

Land Policies

In the early days of the Texas frontier, generous land policies existed to lure new settlers. The Olson family claim in this story of one section, or 640 acres, is based on the policy in place when Norwegians settled in Kaufman and Van Zandt counties. A section is one square mile of land, meaning it forms a square that is one mile (5,280 feet) long on each side. This was more than ten times larger than the average 'large' farm in Norway! After families built a home, had the land surveyed and proved their intention to settle by starting a farm or ranch, the 640 acres was theirs.

Discuss: *By comparison, a football field is just over one acre in size. An average city block varies from 300600 feet on each side. That means a section of land would hold about 600 football fields or 15 city blocks or 68,000 school* *buses. What else can you think of that measures one square mile?*

Indian Raids

The story of Ole Foss' kidnapping in Chapter 4 is based on an actual event, the kidnapping of Ole Nystel in 1867. Native American raids on frontier settlements sometimes resulted in kidnappings and deaths. Women and children were kidnapped as a sort of human pirate treasure. Some remained in the Native American settlements as workers or were adopted into the tribe. Others were kidnapped specifically to be traded back to their families for guns or other goods. Though they were rare in more settled areas, stories of raids were frightening enough to keep many settlers on their guard.

Discuss: *In this story, Ole Foss from Normandy area is kidnapped by Indians, but Kaya's grandmother Olena claims she has never seen an Indian in the 20 years she has lived in Texas. What accounts for this difference?*

Texas Norwegians and the Civil War

Scholars estimate about 100 Norwegians fought for the Confederacy during the Civil War, partly because there weren't that many Norwegians living in the south at the time, and partly because many Norwegians did not wish to fight to support slavery. Of those that did participate, most were from Texas and served in Texas or nearby. Some, like Wilhelm Waerenskjold, served regardless of their anti-slavery beliefs, because their American neighbors mistrusted anyone who did not want to fight for the Confederacy.

Discuss: *Have you ever gone along with something you didn't agree with, just to get along with new friends or neighbors? Is it best to go along, or make your true feelings known?*

Postwar Daily Life

In Chapter 6, Olena Olson mentions how happy she is to have regular newspaper and mail delivery again.

During the Civil War, many common items became scarce. Either their production was interrupted to manufacture items for the war, or their delivery was interrupted by armies on land or blockades by sea. Paper became scarce, so many newspapers ceased production. Fabric was not easily available, so folks had to make their own, known as 'homespun'. The same with coffee and sugar, two items not easily grown in America. Coffee substitutes ranged from common sense items like chicory, to crazy ideas like tree bark and old cigar butts! The cost of sugar rose. One source says a pound of sugar cost $10. Today's equivalent? $153.00. By comparison, my local grocer recently offered a 4 lb bag for $1.99 or about 50 cents a pound. Texas families were at least able to feed themselves with the livestock and produce they raised on their own. Bartering, or trading for items instead of using money, was common. Southerners had money, but it was Confederate money.

Confederate money did not have much value. People

feared if the South lost the war, the money would be

worthless, so no one would take it in exchange for goods or

services.

After the war, life slowly returned to normal.

Newspaper and mail delivery resumed, as did school.

Coffee, sugar and fabric returned to the shelves. Men

returned from the battlefield and resumed work on their

land.

Discuss: *Can you name something that has become unavailable or very costly due to events far away? How did you feel when things returned to normal?*

Children's Roles

During the frontier period, children were an

important part of the pioneer family unit. They were

expected to help in virtually all aspects of frontier life. In a

time when most everything needed was made by hand,

there was little time for play. Chores were divided between boys and girls, with boys doing most of the outside work (tending the animals, farming, building and equipment maintenance) and girls given the indoors jobs (cleaning, cooking, sewing). Children attended school if one was available, but schools closed during harvest time in the fall, since all were needed to help with this important and time-consuming task.

Discuss: *What chores are you responsible for at home? Do you think they should be assigned based on whether you are a boy or a girl?*

Children's Games

One of the central events of this story involves a children's game called a snipe hunt. A snipe hunt is a combination hideandgoseek and April Fool's joke. Frontier children had less time for recreation after school and chores, but they still found ways to have fun. Popular games included races (on foot, on horse, 'wheelbarrow',

and threelegged, to name a few); marbles (sometimes

played with anything small and round, such as acorns); and

horseshoes.

Discuss: *Sometimes the simplest games are the best,
lasting throughout generations. Name some games that are
enjoyed today that require no electricity or other modern
technology.*

Norse Mythology

Kaya's dog is named Odin, after the Norse god

associated with wisdom and knowledge. The ancient Norse

had a complex religion with many gods including Thor,

upon whom the recent movie and comic book character is

based. The popularity of Norse mythology faded as

Christianity spread throughout Europe. By the time

Norwegians began immigrating to America, most had

converted to the Lutheran religion. But their mythology

remained as part of their cultural folklore.

233

Discuss: *What are some other examples of ancient beliefs remaining in your local or family folklore?*

Criminal Activity

The American frontier is often portrayed as a dangerous, lawless place. When she first arrived in Texas in the 1840s, Elise Waerenskjold wrote that most Texans felt perfectly safe and rarely locked their homes because there was no need to steal, meaning everyone had plenty. But the Civil War stirred up animosities, and crimes encroached upon her community. Her husband Wilhelm narrowly avoided death by a lynch mob in 1864 for his antislavery views, only to be murdered in 1866 during a domestic dispute with a neighbor. The postwar surge in crime in north and east Texas inspired the Jesse Spence storyline.

Discuss: *The Texas frontier had its share of infamous outlaws. Can you name any?*

Camp Meetings

As the frontier became settled, some services were slow to arrive. While communities waited for churches to be built and preachers to be assigned to them, they often held services in private homes, led by a community member or 'lay person'. Pastors sometimes had to cover a large area, staying only a few weeks in each place before moving on. A new type of religion evolved using the concept of a traveling religious service known as a camp meeting. Independent preachers roamed the frontier, setting up camps near towns. The meetings lasted for a few days. People came for miles to hear the preacher's sermons and enjoy the singing and fellowship.

Discuss: *What similar traveling outdoor activities can you think of that we still enjoy today?*

Epidemics

Texans in the 1800s experienced many types of epidemics. They did not have the technology to understand or treat illnesses like malaria, yellow fever, measles, or influenza. The 'fever' in this story is based on an actual epidemic that struck the Norwegian community and resulted in many of the survivors moving west to a healthier climate. Frontier settlers often did not have access to doctors or hospitals. Quantities were sometimes limited either due to supply shortages, lack of funds, or both. Settlers relied on their own medical knowledge and home remedies such as herbs, teas, and ointments.

Discuss: *What remedies do you have at home to take when you become injured or feel sick?*

Bibliography

Dallas Times Herald, October 19, 1867.

Norwegian Phrase Book and Dictionary. Oxford, England: Berlitz Publishing Company Ltd., 1990.

Albertson, Dorothy Earle. Mid-Night Sun (Norway) To Texas. Tyler, Texas, 1942.

Anderson, Rasmus B. The First Chapter of Norwegian Immigration, (1821-1840), Its Causes and Results. Madison, Wisconsin, 1896.

Bresenhan, Karoline Patterson, and Nancy O'Bryant Puentes. Lone Stars: A Legacy of Texas Quilts, 1836-1936. Vol. 1. Austin: University of Texas Press, 1986.

Campbell, Randolph B. Grass-roots Reconstruction in Texas, 1865-1880. Baton Rouge: Louisiana State University Press, 1997.

Carson, Bridget and Sue Rhodes, "Tobacco Use During the Civil War" 8 Mar 2006 http://www.shasta.com/suesgoodco/newcivilians/advice/tobacco. htm

Clausen, C. A., ed. The Lady with the Pen: Elise Waerenskjold in Texas. Clifton, Texas: Bosque Memorial Museum, 1976.

Clausen, C. A. & Derwood Johnson. "Norwegian Soldiers in Confederate Forces." Norwegian-American Studies, vol. 25,

Northfield, MN. p. 114.

Englund, Joyce. "The Dala Horse: From Folk Toy to
Lindsborg Tradition." 10 March, 2006
http://www.svenskhyllningsfest.org/dala_horse.htm

Franck, Irene J. The Scandinavian-American Heritage.
New York: Facts on File Publications, 1988.

Grimeland, Jorgen Jorgenson. Letter. 8 April 1856.

The Norwegian Texans. The University of Texas Institute
of Texan Cultures at San Antonio, 1971.

Jenson, Martin T. Four Mile. Dallas, Texas: Roberts
Printing, 1972.

Lovoll, Odd S. The Promise of America: A History of the
Norwegian-American People. Minneapolis: University of
Minnesota Press in cooperation with The Norwegian-American
Historical Association, 1984.

Martin, Nancy J. Threads of Time. Bothell, WA: That
Patchwork Place, 1990.

Mieder, Wolfgang. "The Apple Doesn't Fall Far From the
Tree – A Historical and Contextual Proverb Study Based on
Books, Archives and Databases." De Proverbio Electronic
Journal of International Proverb Studies, v. 1. .n.1 1995.

Moneyhon, Carl. H. Texas After the Civil War: The
Struggle of Reconstruction. TAMU Press, 2004.

Nystel, Ole T. Lost and Found or Three Months with the
Indians.

Refsal, Harley. Woodcarving in the Scandinavian Style.
New York: Sterling Publishing Company, 1992.

Payne, Darwin. "Early Norwegians in Northeast Texas."
Southwest Historical Quarterly, vol. LXV no. 2, October 1962.

Roalson, Louise. Notably Norwegian. Benfield Press,
Iowa City, IA, 1982.

Robinson, Lana. " A Little Bit of Norway." Texas
Highways, September 1984, pp. 18-29.

Robinson, Lana. "Norse, of Course!" Texas Highways,
November 1999, pp. 38-43.

Russell, Charles H. Undaunted: A Norwegian Woman in
Frontier Texas. College Station: Texas A&M Press, 2006.

Semmingsen, Ingrid. Norway to America: A History of the
Migration. Minneapolis: University of Minnesota, 1978.

Smallwood, James. Murder and Mayhem: The War of
Reconstruction in Texas. TAMU 2003.

Stokker, Kathleen. Keeping Christmas: Yuletide Traditions
in Norway and the New Land. St. Paul: Minnesota Historical
Society Press, 2000.

Unstad, Lyder L. "Norwegian Migration to Texas: A
Historic Resume with Four 'America Letters'". Southwestern
Historical Quarterly, vol. III, no. 2, October 1939.

Wisdom, Helen Richman, comp. Prairieville: The Town on
Four Mile Prairie. Gun Barrel City, TX: Graphics Etc., 1996.

About The Author

LISSA JOHNSTON has a Master's degree in
history from the University of Texas at Arlington and is the
author of several non-fiction books for young readers. She
is a proud descendant of the Olson family, who immigrated
from Norway to Texas in the mid-1800s. A Native Texan
and mother of two adult children, Lissa currently lives with
her husband in South Carolina.

Other works by Lissa Johnston:

*Crossing A Continent: The Incredible Journey of Cabeza
de Vaca*
Portraits of the States Series: Alabama
Mary McLeod Bethune: Empowering Educator
Rulers of India
Frida Kahlo: Painter of Strength
Ellen Ochoa: Pioneering Astronaut
*Places in Time Series: A Brief Political and Geographic
History of North America*

Thank You!

Thank you so much for reading! If you like what you read, I hope you will share your comments. I would love to hear from you personally, either via email at lissajohnston@gmail.com, or at my website www.lissajohnston.com. When you visit my site, be sure to subscribe to my newsletter for updates on future projects.

Social networking is great, too.

Facebook
I have both a personal profile and an author page under my name, Lissa Johnston.

Twitter @Lissa_Johnston

Pinterest
I have set up a board for *The Dala Horse*. It's great for helping visualize many of the characters and events from the book. You should be able to find it by searching the title or searching within my boards. If you have any trouble finding it, reach out to me and I'll send you a link.

Book reviews are a great way to help independent authors like myself. If you enjoy *The Dala Horse*, I hope you will take a minute and write a review at Amazon or Goodreads - or both!

Copyright

The Dala Horse
By Lissa Johnston

Copyright © 2015 by Lissa Johnston

Cover Design by www.ebooklaunch.com

ISBN: 978-0-9973068-2-8

Made in the USA
San Bernardino, CA
19 November 2019